Journal
of a
Sneaky Twerp

GREGOR "SHMEGEGGE" HUFFLEPUFF'S MEMOIR

by Jest Ninney

"Parody, therefore, is a form of imitation, but imitation characterized by ironic inversion, not always at the expense of the parodied text. [...] Parody is, in another formulation, repetition with critical distance, which marks difference rather than similarity."

— Linda Hutcheons, A Theory of Parody

"[T]he fair use of a copyrighted work [...] for purposes such as criticism, comment, news reporting, teaching [...] is not an infringement of copyright."

— Limitations on exclusive rights: Fair use, 17 United States Code §107

ISBN-13: 9780980211481

Cover design by: Lalita Euginia

TO MOE, LARRY, GRUMPY, DOPEY,
SLEEZY, AND NURSE RATCHED

WARNING! SYMBOL

HOW GREGOR FEELS
INSIDE

The Journal of a Sneaky Twerp Series

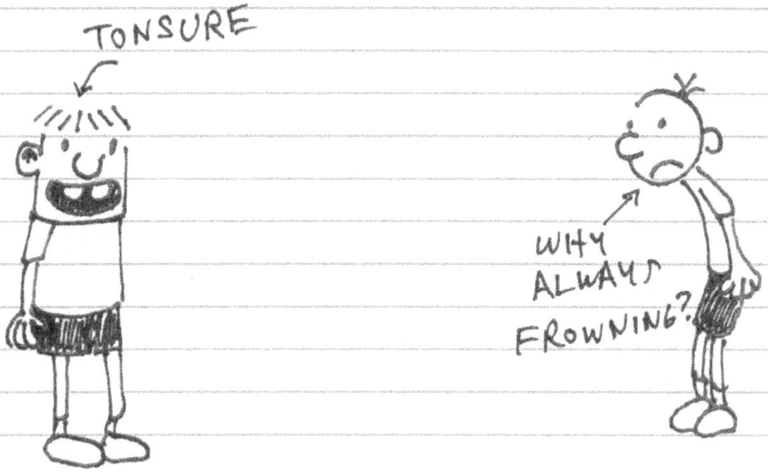
TONSURE
WHY ALWAYS FROWNING?

SEPTEMBER

TUESDAY

Right off the bat, let's clear something up: Why are YOU reading my journal? Are you some sort of weirdo who sneaks into kids' rooms and goes through their personal stuff, like a nosey parent? A journal is private. Put this down right now and walk away.

Oh, I see. You found this book online. Even though it's supposed to be private, I guess I INVITED you to read it. That makes ME the weirdo, not you. I admit it. I'm an EXHIBITIONIST.*

I actually want you to stick your nose into my personal stuff. So this really isn't a journal at all. It's more like a memoir.

* Don't be LAZY. If you don't know what a word means, first try to figure it out by seeing how the word works in the sentence around it. If you can't figure it out, look it up in a dictionary.

Slapdash drawing, like a REAL kid would do.

You're probably not going to like what I have to say here. My Language Arts teacher, Mr. Maass, says that readers seek out books that parrot back to them their own beliefs. No one really wants their morals tested or their minds changed. They just want to feel, when they finish a book, that they were right all along.

So, after all that brow-beating, if you're still with me, here we go.

I worry all the time about how others see me. I'm desperate to be liked. But I REFUSE to talk about my feelings (that's so touchy-feely). IRONICALLY, everything I write about here will be dripping with feelings. Mostly fear. That's called SUBTEXT. You can smell it between the lines.

So now you're my SHRINK, are you? You want to know WHY I like to air my dirty laundry here?

You see, not only am I insecure and lonely, I'm also DELUSIONAL. I make myself feel better by telling myself that one day I'll be rich and famous. Which means, one day I'll be liked—and therefore happy.

Don't ask me what I'll actually DO to become rich and famous. Maybe win the lottery. Or get picked for a hit reality TV show. All I know is that the world owes me fame and fortune because I'm special. This memoir will prove it.

Who am I? I'm an average middle-class white kid from an American suburb. My whole world consists of the cul-de-sac where I live.

I'm also a MISANTHROPE.

Too lazy to look that word up? Fine. It means I hate people. I think anyone who doesn't look or act or talk like me is a weirdo or a moron. You could call this PROJECTION. I project my insecurities onto those around me.

I go to a public middle school. That's the place where non-rich parents send their kids—the ones who are too old to be cute and too young to be interesting. Think of it as taxpayer-funded daycare so parents have a few precious hours to themselves.

The scariest thing about middle school, though, is that some of the older kids here have gone through PUBERTY. That means they're old enough to make babies. These gangly, hairy kids are so scary, to make myself feel better, I have to DEMUHANIZE them by calling them GORILLAS.

Sometimes they bully me. Probably because they smell the fear on me. The way I deal with their bullying is by bullying kids smaller and weaker than me. As my Pops always says, POOP rolls downhill.

If I had my way, I'd drop out of school and go work at a smartphone factory. At least then I could earn some cash to buy candy and video games.

IMMIGRANT
INDIAN RUNT
STEREOTYPE

In middle school, the teachers are supposed to teach us knowledge and skills we'll need someday to be contributing adults. But at this stage, what we study is all so basic. It's things grownups take for granted—like learning how to spell CALENDAR and not to chew with your mouth open.

They make us sit in orderly rows of desks under harsh fluorescent light. We squirm as frustrated grownups talk AT us for six hours a day. The teachers also make us memorize and REGURGITATE a lot of random information. Of course, they never bother to explain why all this boring stuff is worth our attention.

There are a lot of rules we have to follow in school. It's kind of like being in prison or being grounded. I feel trapped. So I find little ways to rebel. Mostly, that means being AGGRESSIVELY PASSIVE, which means refusing to go along with what grownups want me to do.

Another scary thing about middle school is that even before kids go through puberty, they start getting interested in gender and sex. Once I heard an actor on a popular TV show call girls HOT. So now I copy him and call some girls at school HOT. Never to their face, which would be way too scary. Just around my friends so that they can clearly see that I'm not GAY.

You're probably wondering: How does a girl earn, in my book, the label HOT? To be honest, I'm not totally sure. She smiles a lot. She's not fat. She has Goldilocks boobs. Not too big. Not too small. She wears trendy clothes that show off her hips. Basically, it's all about her LOOKS. Because looks are all that matters for girls, right?

I tell everybody I've ALWAYS liked girls. It's not a lie, exactly. More like an exaggeration. I'm just so desperate for everyone to like me that I'm an equal-opportunity suck-up. If I think you're popular, I'm happy to lick your boot, regardless of your gender or sexual-orientation. But if I believe you're less popular than me, I have no problem insulting you for being unlike me, MR. AVERAGE MIDDLE-CLASS AMERICAN WHITE GUY.

But now that I think about it, I don't actually have any friends who are girls. The only girl I talk to regularly is my mom.

But I'm definitely one of those boys who's so OBSESSED with popularity that I take the trouble to rank every kid in school from one all the way down to one hundred and fifty-three.

My best friend Jowley doesn't pay attention to me when I tell him all about the importance of being POPULAR. He still plays like a little kid, which means he's not interested in SOCIAL STATUS or other trappings of acting mature. He's just happy. How boring.

WEDNESDAY

Today we had Phys Ed, which is the only way the government can get us American kids off our LARD-MARBLED duffs. On the other hand, there's a ton of sugar in just about everything we eat and drink and screens everywhere, so it's hard to see how an hour or two of Phys Ed each week is going to make much of a difference.

I bring up Phys Ed because it's a FLIMSY PRETEXT to mention that I went to look at a slice of moldy CHEESE on the four square court. I don't mean to insult your intelligence. I'm sure you're well aware that a slice of cheese would NEVER last that long outside like that. Crows or rats would eat it. What was left would be washed away by the rain or finished off by bugs and bacteria. The cycle of life!

The reason I stuck the cheese here is because it's a SYMBOL. The toxic cheese represents how I feel about myself. I'm always afraid I have the CHEESE TOUCH, which is a fancy middle-school way of saying that I'm afraid I have cooties. I really want kids to like me, but I always worry that they see me as unworthy.

Like I said, there's really no way for me to avoid feeling like I have the Cheese Touch. I'd tell you I cross my fingers to block it. But, again, that'd be insulting to you, dear reader. 'Cause then you'd see I was making one thing up to cancel something else I ALSO made up. A lot of worries are like that.

I might even make a joke about how crossing my fingers all the time to ward off the Cheese Touch made me get a bad grade in handwriting. But then you'd think I was the one who was a

MORON, since I could've just crossed the fingers on my non-writing hand.

But don't you see? My little joke is kind of INADVERTENTLY clever. I worry so much about popularity that my grades suffer.

Then again, the whole idea of GRADES is stupid, isn't it?

Why do grownups make kids chase grades in school? Shouldn't students want to learn for the fun and satisfaction of it? All chasing grades does is have kids grow up looking to authority figures for the motivation to achieve things. Chasing approval like sheep, instead of expressing their own innate creativity.

THURSDAY

Summer is rough. You go from being imprisoned at school to being stuck at home. Another dumb American tradition that's long past its expiration date. Parents still have to work, don't they? So what do they do for daycare? If they're lucky, they can send their kids to the grandparents. If not, they send them to camps—basically, school with less supervision and more bullying. Or worse, they leave them home—to spend their days playing video games and eating sugary snacks. That's what my family does.

It'd be great, except that my older brother, Cowlick, is home too. He's an important ANTAGONIST in my story. An antagonist is someone the PROTAGONIST (or hero) of the story fights with. Actually, everybody in my story is an antagonist of some sort, including myself. That's because I'm my own worst enemy.

Remember how my Pops said that poop runs downhill. Cowlick is the oldest sibling. He's a teenager. So he's uphill from me. And Cowlick is kind of SADISTIC. He likes to play pranks on me. In his mind, the more cruel the better.

I'd tell you he tricked me one time in July into thinking it was a school morning when it was actually the middle of the night. But that wouldn't be very original.

Cowlick is a GENIUS when it comes to pranks. One time he got me deported to Mexico. He hid my birth certificate and social security card and convinced some ICE agents who were hanging around the playground that I was a bilingual *criollo* DREAMER. ICE held me in a detention camp on the border for three months before my parents were able to get me released. But only after they'd spent tens of thousands of dollars on immigration lawyers and wrote a personal appeal to the President himself. And they never did pin the scam on Cowlick.

See what I mean? A genius.

FRIDAY

At school this morning, our teacher put us in reading groups.

There are two kinds of people in this world—dummies and smarty-pants. The dummies have it much easier than the smarty-pants. No one expects anything from them. So they get to do what they like.

In contrast, parents and teachers expect the world of the smarty-pants. Get straight As. Go to a top college. Become a doctor, lawyer, or engineer, maybe even President. That's a lot of pressure. And a lot of work.

I'm lazy. I'd rather get an easy job where my boss doesn't expect much from me—or better yet, where I'm my own boss and can goof off all day and no one will notice or even care. Like President.

So I always look for ways to show off how dumb I am. One way is to try things that you can get good at with a ton of effort—like writing novels or playing the piano. Of course, since I'm a beginner, my initial results are really bad. Then I get frustrated and give up.

So all I have to show for myself is a bunch of crappy work from a bunch of different things I try for, like, a minute, then give up on. I think this is an excellent plan for getting nowhere in life. Which is just where I want to be.

In spite of all my schemes, Mummy still thinks I'm super smart. She says I just don't "apply" myself. That makes it sound like I'm a coat of paint.

But Mummy must not be too smart herself. Otherwise, she'd wonder what it is she's doing as a parent that makes me so uninterested in giving things my best effort.

Of course, there are times when I do like people to think I'm smart. Like when I make brilliant jokes about how dumb kids are sooo dumb they don't even know how to hold a book the right way.

SATURDAY

The first week of school is over. I like to sleep in on the weekends. Also, I like to take a lot of naps. I would stay in bed all day, if I could. Mummy worries that I sleep all the time because I'm CLINICALLY DEPRESSED.

I don't know why she thinks that. I'm not depressed. I just hate everybody, including myself, and feel like life has no meaning.

She says I should go see a shrink and get some happy pills. But I don't really like taking medicine. I'd rather just sleep or play video games all day. That's the best medicine for what ails me.

Pops tries to get me out of bed in the morning by throwing a bucket of ice water on my head. He says the best way to get excited about life is to work out or do sports. He says that if I continue to waste my life away in bed, he'll send me to a military academy. That sounds like fun. I hear they teach you how to shoot people there.

I finally got out of bed and went to my BFF Jowley's house. Jowley is the only kid in my school who's oblivious enough to put up with all my selfish nonsense. He doesn't mind that I just use him as a sounding board for all my crazy schemes. He doesn't even mind that I'm always super-embarrassed by everything he says and does. I think it's totally because of him—the ridiculous things he's always saying and doing. I never stop to think that maybe it's because I'm terrified about how others see me.

For example, we were hanging out by our lockers today when Jowley asked me if I wanted to come over to his house after school and "play." That's what little kids do. They play. Cool middle-school kids "hang out."

Who wants to enjoy life by using our imaginations freely? I'd rather worry about what other people think about me, come up with ways of tricking them into liking me, and when I'm not doing that, mope around or busy myself with mindlessly addictive activities that help me temporarily forget my own self-loathing.

Like I said, the thing I like best about Jowley is that he lets me use him. When Cowlick bullies me, I take what he did to me and use it on Jowley. I'm always finding ways to humiliate Jowley by making him the brunt of a cruel prank. It's fun!

MONDAY

Remember how I said I like to play dumb so I don't have to try at anything? Well, sometimes I really am just plain stupid.

Here's an example. I have a little brother. His name is Fanny. (See. If this were a real diary, I wouldn't bother explaining this, since I know I have a little brother named Fanny. Duh.)

I think it's really unfair that Fanny gets away with stuff that would get me into big trouble. That's how dumb I am. I'm not at all aware that behavioral expectations are relative to a child's cognitive development. I just want to treat Fanny like my equal even though he's a toddler.

Anyways, according to the IRON LAW of poop rolling downhill, I should be able to bully Fanny just like I bully Jowley, since he's weaker than me.

But for some inexplicable reason, Mummy and Pops protect Fanny from me. Not only that, they try to teach me responsibility by making me take care of Fanny. I have to make him breakfast. Never mind that they let me feed him sugary cereal. Never mind that they let me plop him in front of a TV while he eats.

They also make me clean up the mess he makes when he gets a sugar rush and acts out the cartoon violence he sees on the TV. And they say I'm the one being irresponsible.

Even though I'm mean to Fanny, he still likes me. Which I don't get. He came up with a cute name for me when he was very little and couldn't pronounce words like "brother." He still calls me "Butter." Of course, I'm so insecure, I don't see how endearing this is. It's just another thing for me to be embarrassed about. But you do. That makes you feel superior to me.

TUESDAY

The thing I'm most proud of about myself is that I'm really good at playing video games. Like most kids, I have a delusional sense of my own potential and a dim grasp of probabilities, so I believe I will be a professional gamer in the future.

But my parents won't let me. They say it's enough that I spend all my free time playing video games. They don't want to have to drive me to tournaments and manage my career for me. Apparently, they've never heard of the internet and that you can do all of that from the comfort of your sofa.

Mummy and Pops don't like it when I hog the TV, though. Pops want to watch Wolf News, Mummy, Peacock News. All day, every day. So Pops sometimes kicks me out of the house. He tells me to go out and get some exercise. Maybe do some marching drills or target practice.

I'd say that if Pops really wanted to, he could just unplug my video game console and sell it on Ebay. I definitely wouldn't say he's too dumb to figure out how to unplug a console, though. Because that'd be a pretty lame joke, wouldn't it?

Instead, I wonder why my parents don't just forbid me from playing video games altogether. Or at the very least, make a rule where I can only play one hour a day, after I do my homework. I guess they let me play video games as much as I want because it's a really cheap babysitter. They can check out as parents while I check out from the real world.

When Pops kicks me out of the house, I go to Jowley's house to play video games there. I guess his mom likes to check out too. But she likes to think she's a great parent because she screens the games Jowley is allowed to play.

Only games with realistic violence, the gorier the better. His mom says being exposed to so much violence at such a young age will prepare us to fight all the bad guys in the world when we grow up. If a shooter ever attacks our school, we'll be able to defend ourselves and save our cowering classmates because we know how to use a virtual AK-47.

Addressing the root causes.

I get sick of blowing holes in the heads of terrorists with Jowley, though, because he's too serious of a gamer. Jowley wants to talk about their point-of-view, their feelings, whether they have families and friends, whether their cause is justified. I just want to DEHUMANIZE them so it's easy to murder them and not give it a second thought.

This afternoon, after I'd slaughtered a battalion or two of North Koreans, on my way home, I smeared some mud on my face and clothes to make it look like I'd been getting a lot of exercise. That's because the thing I like most to do in life is lie to my parents. The more desperate the deceit, the better.

Don't hurt me. I'm just doing my job.

Unfortunately, Pops didn't notice me when I walked in through the living room looking like a homeless person. He was too busy watching Wolf News. They tell viewers to look down on the poor because it's their own fault they're poor.

WEDNESDAY

You're probably wondering when the INCITING INCIDENT is going to happen. That's the event that kickstarts the story and sends it hurtling toward its inevitable climax.

You've read a lot of novels. You've seen a lot of movies. You have a strong intuition that every good story must contain, as my English teacher Mr. Truby says, the following seven ingredients: a weakness, a desire, an opponent, a plan, a battle, a self-revelation, and a new equilibrium.

So far, you've met the protagonist—that's me—and learned that he does indeed have a big weakness. Actually, I have two that are related: one, I'm insecure; and two, I'm a terrible friend. We can all agree on that, can't we?

You've also learned that I have a strong desire, which is also related to my weakness: I desperately want to be popular.

My opponent? Opponents, actually. I'm pretty much at odds with everybody else in the story. Mummy and Pops, Cowlick, Fanny, and Jowley too.

Who's my main opponent then (otherwise known as the antagonist)? Probably Jowley, since he's my BFF, even though I treat him so poorly. That would make this a BUDDY ROMANCE.

The real antagonist of my story, though, is inside me. It's my insecurity. So it's also a COMING-OF-AGE story. Also, because figuring out how to be a good friend to him will basically take care of my glaring weakness. That's the self-revelation this story is heading towards. Some big sacrifice on my part that shows I've learned how to be a loyal friend.

So what's my plan? I don't really have one. That's why this story feels like it drags in the middle. It's just one scheme that backfires after another. I'm warning you. It feels episodic. So bear with me as I ramble.

Here's yet another opponent—Freckly. He's this weird kid that wants to show me his private parts. I use him as an example of what I definitely don't want to be. He's the exact opposite of popular.

Since Jowley is the main external antagonist, he needs to show up a lot in the plot. So today I'm deciding to go to his house again after school. The reason is another of my opponents has driven me out of the house. Cowlick is practicing with the other members of his quartet. Cowlick plays the violin. But that's not very cool.

So I like to fantasize that he plays the drums and heads a death metal band called Hunny Buckit. They spell it wrong to be cool. Also, it's cool to allude to excrement.

But actually Cowlick calls his quartet Angel Agape. They play baroque chamber music. I hate it. It's like nails being raked down a blackboard.

Fans of Cowlick's quartet.

I don't have any taste in music yet. Basically, I'll listen to whatever's trending on the streaming service Autotunified. I'm not worried. I've got time. It's not until sixth or seventh grade when kids start expecting you to like this band or hate that one. Right now, I can get away with saying I like both kinds of music, Country AND Western.

Mummy wishes music would bring the family together. But everybody knows that kids don't want to share their music with boring, embarrassing grownups. For kids, musical taste is one of the many ways they ham-fistedly try to be independent.

THURSDAY

One way I like to rebel is by listening to and looking at things that are meant only for adults. Luckily, the companies that sell this illicit stuff slap "Parental Warning" or "Rated R" tags on them so they get filtered out of internet browsers with the child locks turned on.

But it's so much fun to be exposed to swearing, violence, nudity, sex, and other "mature" content. You can never grow up too soon. That's my motto.

Anyway, as I said, I like to be sneaky too. The internet makes that a lot easier. I log onto the computer with Pop's easy-to-guess password. Then, after I've browsed all the nasty stuff online, I erase the browsing history, and presto, nobody's any the wiser.

Mummy and Pops refuse to give me a smartphone. They say I'm too young. But, of course, they gave Cowlick one. His passcode is easy to hack too. Sometimes I steal his phone and bring it to school.

Luckily, our school administration is so mediocre, the only time we're not allowed to use smartphones is during class. A lot of the time, though, kids ignore that rule too, and the teachers do nothing. But I like to be extra cautious. I get Jowley to sneak off with me behind the school building so we can listen on the headphones to some "Parental Warning" stuff.

So when our social studies teacher Mrs. Krabappel caught us back there, she just shrugged her shoulders and asked us what we were listening to. I had to think quick. I said, OPP Stale Air. She scowled and said such "middle-brow journalism" would rot our brains.

Jowley started blubbering and saying it was how he kept up with the news of the world. Mrs. Krabappel scoffed and said the news was just "OFFICIOUS GOSSIP" meant to whip the semi-literate masses into a frenzy of anxiety and outrage so corporations could sell them more useless products.

Sometimes I don't know about that kid.

FRIDAY

One time I forgot to erase Pops's browsing history and he got
into a lot of trouble when Mummy found out he was looking at
"mature" stuff she didn't think he should. He sniffed something was
up so he changed his password to something more secure. When I
tried to hack it again, he caught me red-handed.

That month Mrs. Krabappel was teaching us about "parenting
styles." She says there are basically two: "strict father" and
"nurturing mother."

Strict Father parenting happens in a family where the father is in charge. He sits at the top of the pecking order. Everybody beneath him must respect him. In a world seen as fundamentally dangerous, his job is to protect us and teach us how to be self-disciplined. If you disobey him, you get punished, usually through some form of physical violence, like slapping or spanking.

With Nurturing Mother parenting, everyone is treated equally. In a world seen as fundamentally safe, the parents' role is to love and support the children so they grow up to be open-minded, happy adults. Instead of obedience, rules in the house are made through conversation and consensus. Nurturing Mother parents never hit their kids.

Of course, Strict Father parents think Nurturing Mother parents as too mushy and permissive. Nurturing Mother parents see Strict Father types as bullies and tyrants.

Mrs. Krabappel says all of society is organized loosely into these two competing MOIETIES. In our political system, we call them Republicans and Democrats.

One thing's for sure. Mummy is in the Nurturing Mother camp and Pops is a Strict Father, or, at least, that's his inclination. But Mummy rules the roost. So Pops can only exercise his Strict Father parenting style when she's not around. If I break a rule or do something wrong, he'll threaten violence, without actually going through with it.

It makes for a weird relationship. I need him, but I also fear him. I guess that's why I'm so sneaky.

Even though Mummy makes most of the parenting decisions, it feels like she's still on the fence with all this nurturing stuff, though. When her frustration boils over, she does strict things. She use to gave me "time outs." And now that I'm older, she grounds me.

I'm not afraid of Mummy, but her being so understanding all the time can sometimes feel really suffocating.

In the end, Mummy and Pops decided to imprison me for two whole weeks. Isn't it weird—and barbaric—that to punish people who don't follow the big rules in our society, we lock them in cages?

MONDAY

Cowlick's also in trouble with Mummy right now. Fanny got ahold of a box of Cowlick's marijuana gummies and brought it to pre-school. The teacher was about to ask Fanny to share the treats he'd brought with him to school, when she noticed the "Parental Warning" label.

But it was too late. Fanny had already shared them with his classmates. In a half hour, the kids were all rolling around on the carpet, frothing at the mouth and croaking, "the horror, the horror."

The director reported the incident to the police. Luckily, Mummy got off with only probation and six bazillion hours of community service.

Of course, Mummy was furious, just furious with Cowlick for, like, a year. He didn't help his case when he said it was the manufacturer's fault. How stupid was it to make dangerous drugs in the form of candy?

Grownups sure are trying their hardest to make the world as dangerous a place as they can.

Cowlick's punishment was that he had to volunteer at the preschool for a month and potty-train all the kids.

WEDNESDAY

Part of being grounded is that I can't kill time by binging on video games. But, oh boy, I DO get to watch Fanny play as many of his own video games as HE wants. Unfortunately, Fanny is too little to know which video games are good. He pretty much accepts whatever crappy educational games our folks give him. And they're not too discerning. As long as it has a label on it that flatters their aspirational middle-brow tastes, they're all in. BABY NEWTON is their favorite.

I'm at that age where I know all the answers to the questions posed to Fanny by the game. It's also the age, though, where I'm too self-centered to see that these questions are so easy because they're NOT MEANT FOR ME. I just can't help it. I feel compelled to compete with Fanny. So I bark out each answer before he has a chance to think about it.

The good news is that since my folks are so checked out all the time, I can sneak in a few hours of game playing here and there, as long as I keep a good lookout.

THURSDAY

Today at school, the Principal announced the election date for student government. If you're not familiar, student government is where a dictatorship allows its citizens to be in charge of some trivial decisions about their own lives so they have the illusion of control and won't revolt. You could say that about most democracies, really, including our own.

But the cool thing about student elections is that since most of the student "citizens" are so clueless about how it all works, if you run for office and win, you can abuse your power to improve your social status. And since I'm so desperate for social status, I should totally run for office.

Here's my twist. There's too much competition for the high profile positions of President and Vice President. So I'm going to run for Class Secretary. No one wants that position because they think secretaries are ditzy ladies who answer the office phone and type up letters for creepy bosses.

They don't realize that the Class Secretary is the person in charge of all the official record keeping for student government business. It doesn't matter what the President or anyone else decides during our meetings. Whatever I write down from the meeting becomes the official record. That means I'll be the one who's really in charge, ruling behind a curtain like the Wizard of Oz or the author of a book.

So how will I use my power to get more popular? By doling out gifts with expectation of QUID PRO QUO, of course. Which is another way of saying I'll steal from the commonwealth to enrich myself. It's the American Way.

Since I only think of people in terms of crudely gendered stereotypes, the one clique I plan to suck up to is the cheerleaders, since they're all "hot" girls. As I've said, it's very important that not only all the other kids I know but also you, dear reader, think of me as STRAIGHT.

Pompom or pregnant?

For good measure, I also plan to persecute the group the cheerleaders prefer to pick on, the nerds. And while I'm at it, I'll abuse my power to hurt the jocks too, because they're my main rivals to win the affection of the cheerleaders. See? I have it all figured out.

FRIDAY

Today I signed up to run for Class Secretary. I saw, though, that this kid named Generic Anglo-Sounding Name was also running, and he types eighty words per minute. So I'll have to find some other way to rig the election.

I told Pops I was running for student government, and he got pretty serious. He said that politics is a nasty business. To win, I had to be ruthless. It turns out he was President of his middle school back in the day. He said he won because he hired a bunch of GEARHEADS to beat up anybody who didn't vote for him.

He also said you can't get away with such obvious ways of cheating these days. So you have to be smart about it. One way is to focus your campaign on SIMPLISTIC SLOGANS, FALSE PROMISES, and AD HOMINEM ATTACKS on your opponents. The reason, he said, is that voters are really ignorant and only find the political equivalent of JUNK FOOD appealing.

MONDAY

I had a better idea. But I needed a platform. So Pops helped me set up a FACEPLANT page and a POLITICAL ACTION COMMITTEE for my campaign. Then he got my rich uncle to anonymously donate a million dollars to my PAC, which Pops assured him he could claim as a tax write-off, whatever that is. For that amount, Pops promised him his company would be awarded the upcoming soda and candy vending machine contract with the school district. Quid pro quo.

I spent all weekend—at least, when I wasn't playing video games—working on my marketing plan. It centered around Faceplant ads. Early this morning I posted them to Faceplant and turned on the campaign, targeting all the kids in my school.

This kind of microtargeting is what Faceplant is really good at, because their highly profitable business model is to offer a free service to lots of people, spy on them, then sell their personal info to advertisers. Users are the product.

Faceplant also invests a ton of their profits into fine-tuning their targeting algorithms so they get better and better at manipulating users into clicking or clucking or whatever else the advertisers want them to do.

The ads were basically long form essays explaining in detail my positions on key issues facing the class, as well as substantive policy prescriptions.

But after only a couple minutes, Faceplant shut down my campaign. They said it was due to user complaints. It also violated their terms of use. Turns out Faceplant doesn't allow, in their words, the "dissemination of intellectually rigorous, fact-based claims." Only gossip and BS are permitted.

So I guess my political career is officially over.

OCTOBER

MONDAY

October at last!

You probably noticed I'm modeling my story loosely on daily journal entries. This makes it feel more like a real journal. But, like I said, since I have no intention of keeping this thing private, what I'm really writing is a memoir.

Memoirs don't follow such a rigid structure. They're more like novels. If I'd realized this with that *other* version of my story out there, it might've made it feel less episodic. That is, less like a tedious sequence of AND THEN, AND THEN, AND THEN. Or to describe the BEATS of the story another way: scam foiled, scam foiled, scam foiled Ö sacrifice.

So it's a novel in only the laziest sense of the term. There are no insights, no self-revelations. In fact, it's more like a cartoon in novel form, not a "novel in cartoons."

I digress. Where was I?

And then, October.

Only thirty days left before my favorite holiday, Halloween.

Kids like me do that a lot. They fixate on some special treat in the future and count the days until it arrives. Then they hastily consume the treat. Immediately afterwards, they fixate on the next craving and start counting the days all over again. Come to think of it, grownups are a lot like that too. Living for the future.

Of course, we all know Halloween is so appealing to kids because it's yet another excuse to suck down a bunch of sugar. Also, we get to dress up in costumes, which lets us fantasize about what we might be, rather than what we are. It promises an exciting alternative to our boring old selves.

Halloween is also great for the economy—especially for the candy makers and the companies, like DIZZKNEE and WARNHER BROTHERS, that sell intellectual property in the form of superhero and movie character costumes.

Mummy says I'm getting too old to go trick-or-treating. But I prefer to cling to my childhood for as long as possible.

Pops loves Halloween too. He uses it as a pretext to work out unresolved issues from high school. He got bullied a lot back then. So now Halloween is the one time a year he gets to harass high school kids in a way that's more or less socially acceptable. I guess it makes him feel better to get revenge in this way. Of course, all he ends up doing is traumatizing the high school kids he bullies. They, in turn, traumatize those, like me, who are weaker than them. Paying it forward, I guess.

Come to think of it, what happens at the end of this story is totally Pops's fault.

Tonight Mummy took me and Jowley to the Generic Public High School haunted house. Jowley showed up wearing his Warnher Brothers trademarked superhero costume.

This was extremely embarrassing for me. Even though I want all the benefits of being a kid, like free candy, I'm super-sensitive about FITTING IN. Which means not doing anything other kids in my peer group might make fun of me for.

As you know, we kids are very judgmental. We put a lot of pressure on each other to conform. The funny thing is, we have such unformed, and quite honestly, terrible taste, the things we make each other do can seem—I've heard adults point out—pretty ridiculous.

Pops and Mummy are ALWAYS reminding me of that. When they do, I just roll my eyes. Why do they have to be so judgy about us being so judgy?

Anyway, Jowley is so comfortable in his own skin in this sweet, innocent way, it makes me squirm. I just have to find ways to make him feel the way I do.

Teenagers—Cowlick being no exception—love to be scared. They basically fund the horror movie and amusement park industries. I guess it's because they're desperate to escape, even for a fleeting moment, the torment of their own minds.

Since I look up to teenagers, I want to enjoy being scared too. But to be honest, there's a reason why middle-grade novels and movies don't have a lot of realistic violence in them.

My English teacher from last year, Mr. Stine, said that middle graders have to know a story is a fantasy. The real world can't interfere. There's no divorce. No guns. No one ever dies. For teenagers like Cowlick, he said, it's the opposite. The story has to be very real. They have to believe THIS IS HAPPENING.

So in the haunted house, when a fat old guy with an ORANGE FACE, a bad COMBOVER, and a FLAG PIN screamed he was going to LOCK ME UP, it was too much. Me and Jowley started running. But Mummy stepped in and saved us.

Pops says the best way to get bullies to stop being mean is to make them the center of attention. That's really what they crave— adoration. So he invited the fat old guy to be President, and everything went smoothly in the haunted house after that.

SATURDAY

The haunted house gave me an idea. A great way to be popular these days is to start a business. Young men who start businesses are called BROPRENEURS. And it's pretty much guaranteed that when you found a startup, if it's cool, it'll grow into what's called a UNICORN and you'll be worth a billion bucks. Then everybody will love you. And you'll love yourself, because self-worth correlates strongly with net worth. It's called FINANCIAL FREEDOM, the only real freedom.

The guys who ran the Generic High School haunted house were charging twenty bucks a pop, and the line stretched around the block. They'd be billionaires in no time. And for BROPRENEURS, billionaires are like DEMIGODS.

I bet I could make a killing with my own haunted house franchise. Since I compulsively need others' approval, I decided to let Jowley in on the scheme. Not only that, because I'm such a generous guy, I offered to have Jowley take on most of the risk. We'd build the haunted house in HIS basement.

We came up with an awesome plan:

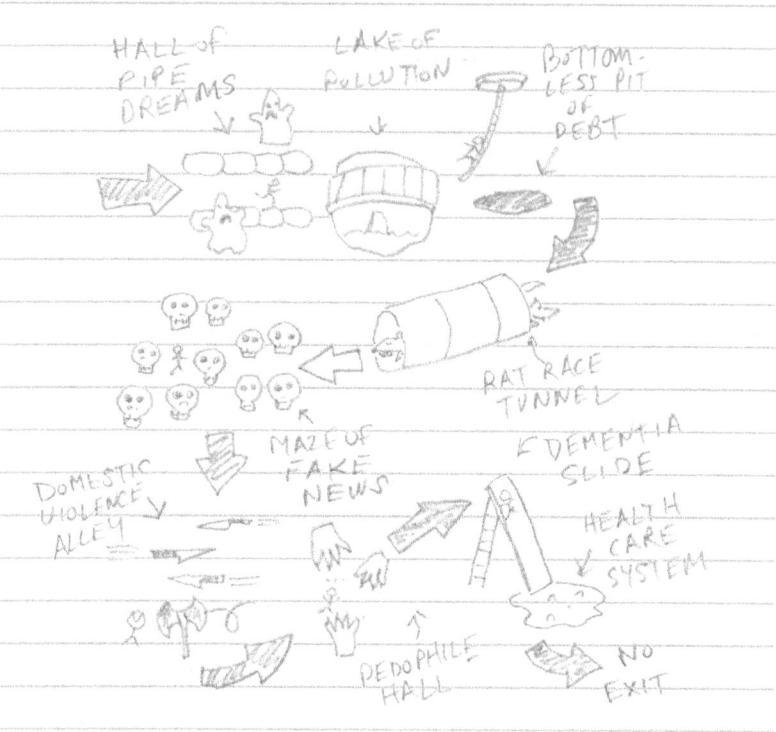

I'm a pretty humble guy, so I don't usually brag. But our—really my—haunted house was waaay better than the one at Generic High School.

Now we needed to get the word out. So we stapled up a bunch of flyers around the neighborhood.

After the election disaster, Mrs. Krabappel told me the most effective advertising has 3 key elements—a promise, a pitch, and a price. The promise tells your prospects HOW what's on offer will change their life for the better. The pitch explains WHY they should buy now. And the price is, well, how much it costs.

So this is what we—I mean I—came up with:

When we finished putting up all the flyers, we only had an hour before the haunted house was supposed to open. So we had to adjust our master plan.

You're probably wondering why Jowley's mom failed to notice all the hubbub going on down in her basement. Just to let you know, Jowley only has his mom because his parents are divorced. His dad lives in Phuket with his new "girlfriend." Jowley sees him twice a year, for Christmas and during summer vacation. And his mom works a lot. So basically Jowley is a latch-key kid.

When it was time to open the haunted house, we went outside. A couple dozen kids had shown up. I decided to UPSELL them on some exclusive features. Also, we doubled the entry fee for half of them, based on their ability to pay. It's called DYNAMIC PRICING.

But when our customers got down to the basement and saw in the black light only a few pillows thrown around, they realized they'd been ripped off. They demanded a refund. We insisted all sales were final. A scuffle broke out.

Just then, Jowley's mom came home. She made us give all their money back. And she made us pay her a penalty for what she called FRAUD. I had to give her all my birthday money from the past three years. She used it to buy a new pair of LOOBOOTAWNS. So we scammers wound up getting scammed by more powerful scammers.

She said that's how the world works, so get used to it.

SUNDAY

Jowley's mom grounded him for a week. He wasn't even allowed to read the dictionary, which is his favorite hobby, besides pruning his Bonsai tree.

To make him feel better, I stole Cowlick's phone again and read the dictionary out loud to him.

scapegoat, n., 1. In the Mosaic ritual of the Day of Atonement (Lev. xvi), that one of two goats that was chosen by lot to be sent alive into the wilderness, the sins of the people having been symbolically laid upon it, while the other was appointed to be sacrificed.

—Oxford English Dictionary

I have to confess: my editor told me to put this scene in here. To show that I'm not a total monster. That sometimes I do nice things for Jowley. That we have a REAL friendship. It's not just me using him for company until I can upgrade to a more popular group of friends.

You see, my editor said it's important to show this now, so that later, when I make my big sacrifice for Jowley, you'll be moved. That's the theory, anyway.

TUESDAY

Halloween is finally here! I'm so excited to gorge myself on candy for a couple weeks. Pops keeps joking that if I keep eating so much sugar, I'm going to get TYPE II DIABETES. Well, I think he's half serious about it. My uncle has diabetes, and he has to take insulin shots all the time.

I don't like shots. Really, I don't like any kind of pain whatsoever. I try to avoid it at all costs. And when I know something painful is about to happen, I get so squirmy it makes the pain much worse. Pops says that's because imagined pain is much worse than actual physical pain. It's called suffering.

Cowlick just tells me to stop being such a BABY and suck it up. But he doesn't understand. I'm all about making sure I enjoy pleasure and avoid pain not only now, but more importantly, IN THE FUTURE.

Anyways, I've been anticipating Halloween for a whole month. And when Halloween is over, I'll immediately start looking forward to Christmas.

Every year, my folks insist I buy my Halloween costume from a big box store. Mummy says buying as much stuff as we can charge on credit is good for the economy. It creates lots of low-wage service jobs, like cashiers and stocking clerks. It also helps China by giving peasants there a chance to earn—what for them is—a princely sum by working 12 hours a day, 6 days a week in a factory.

Not only that, but buying then throwing away lots of cheap consumer goods warms the climate. With a warmer climate, we don't have to shovel snow from the driveway in the winter. And there's a lot more days off from school because of hurricanes and forest fires. It's a win for everybody.

But Cowlick thinks it's lame to wear store-bought costumes. They're always based on superheroes and popular movie characters. Which means by wanting to be those characters you're just enriching the corporations that own the trademarks.

The coolest costumes, he says, imitate those brands but comment on them IRONICALLY. This year he's going as OVERMAN, a rip-off of Superman that calls attention to the fact that the creators of Superman stole their idea from this old German philosopher named KNEECHEE or something.

That's a lot of pressure. I'm just going to throw a sheet over my head and say I'm a ghost. Besides, I never want my costume to be too well planned out. The other kids will get ENVIOUS and make fun of me. That's because the crowd always hates it when one of their members stands out too much.

On top of that, trying something original is a big risk because your audience might not get it and just think your costume is OBSCURE. Nobody wants to think too hard about anything. That's especially true for the grownups who dole out the candy on Halloween. You know your costume is TOO clever, when they have to ask you what you're going as. Whatever your answer is, they just give you a high-pitched compliment like "interesting" or "neat-o." But what they really mean is THIS KID IS WEIRD or THE TRULY NEW TERRIFIES ME.

On the other hand, when they're scared, they're more likely to give you a lot of candy just to get rid of you. It's a bribe so you don't opt to play a trick on them.

HALLOWEEN

After a ton of back and forth, I decided to steal Cowlick's idea and go as a pirate. Not the old fashioned kind with an eyepatch and hook for a hand. A modern pirate who videotapes blockbuster movies in the theater and posts them on BITTORRENT for everyone to enjoy for free. It's an easy costume to make. I just wear a black t-shirt with a Russian flag decal and pizza stains on it, a headset, and hold a can of energy drink.

I have to hand it to Jowley. He went as the one thing that scares Americans more than anything else in the world—a HOMELESS FENTANYL-DEALING ILLEGAL IMMIGRANT JIHADIST.

As you know, in a comedy the protagonist is set up over and over again to fall. It's called the COMIC NIGHTMARE. In good comedy, each nightmare attacks the hero's main weakness, and they get more and more intense as the story goes on.

In all stories, the protagonist has a plan to get what he wants. But in comedy, the plan is often a SCAM. My scam for Halloween is to put as little effort as possible into my costume, go out trick-or-treating with ONLY Jowley, and hit as many houses as we can so we land a HUGE candy haul.

But then the nightmare descends.

I was tempted to write that Mummy wanted us to take Fanny and Pops with us. What a nightmare. Having to go with my insufferable family. That means slightly less candy, which is to say, still more candy than I could possibly eat in one or two sittings. What a disaster for kid whose whole world is a cul-de-sac.

When we finally got rid of the intrusive parents and little kids, Jowley told me he needed to pee. The nerve of that kid. How dare he have bodily needs!

Pops says Paris has these cool things called PISSOIRS out on the streets everywhere. He says they put them there a long time ago because the men were drunk all the time and had to go potty, like, every two seconds. Mummy says it's yet one more example of MALE PRIVILEGE.

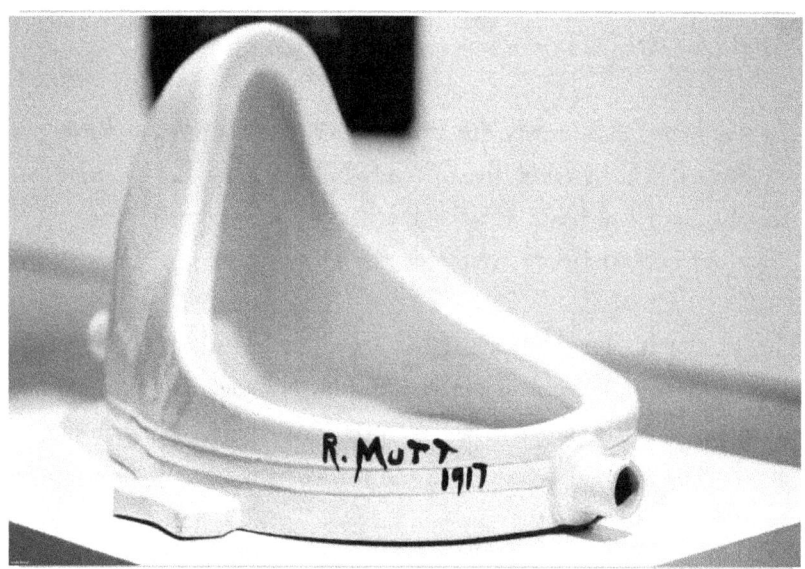

The French elevate pissing to fine art.

Unfortunately, our neighborhood doesn't have any pissoirs. All the homeowners resent having to pay property taxes. They say it's just the government stealing their hard-earned money and giving it away to moochers. So there are no funds for community services like public bathrooms.

I was going to write that Jowley insisted he ask one of the grownups giving out treats if he could use their bathroom. But all grownups know that boys in middle school have terrible aim. They'd never let either of us anywhere near their PRISTINE toilets. Besides, even though there are no pissoirs around, we have the next best thing—bushes.

Whoops. He had to go NUMBER TWO too. No big deal. The neighborhood dogs will clean it up for us, if you know what I mean.

Anyways, by the time we got Jowley all sorted out, it was late. No one would answer their doorbells. No treats. So we were obliged to play a trick on them. Luckily, I swiped some things from home that came in handy. Eggs, dog poop, paper bags, a lighter, toilet paper rolls, a jar of cockroaches, a couple cans of spray paint, rocks to stick in car exhaust pipes, fake audit notices from the IRS, and the COUP-DE-GRACE, Cowlick's smartphone so we could call 911.

There's this grumpy old man named Mr. Hannity who lives in a McMansion on NIMBY Road. He gave us apples. The nerve. So we SWATTED him. Look that up.

Alright. I'll save you the trouble.

When someone calls in a make-believe hostage situation or other major offense that would need to be handled by a SWAT team. Mostly done to streamers mid broadcast or other famous Youtube/Twitch celebrities.

—Urbane Dictionary

Remember how I keep saying poop rolls downhill. Pops traumatized teens by squirting battery acid on their faces. Now those same teens were driving around in an electric car looking to pick on weaker kids.

As part of his costume, Jowley was wearing a mink coat. Apparently, these teens were passionate ANIMAL ACTIVISTS. They splashed him in pig's blood. When their car zipped silently away, I shouted something I quickly came to regret.

The car turned around. They were going to turn us into ROADKILL. We started running. Jowley thought we should cut through a backyard. But I told him they shoot trespassers in this neighborhood. I'd write that we took shelter in my grandma's home, but Mummy put her in a nursing home a long time ago, because of her DEMENTIA and a long list of COMORBIDITIES.

So we had to make a run for it back to my house. It was easy to ditch them because they had to stay on the roads. It was also dark. They couldn't really see us because town hall had turned off all the street lamps due to budget cutbacks.

I'd write that just as we got back to my house and thought we were safe, Pops, thinking we were teens, splashed acid on us. But that would insult your intelligence, wouldn't it? First off, it was late. All the trick-or-treaters had long since gone home. The teens that remained were partying in the convenience store parking lot. Also, he would have known it was us right away. He's not blind.

Anyway, we went inside and did an inventory of our candy haul. Mummy tried to get me to trade it all in for a SWITCH WITCH prize. She said she'd get me my own smartphone. So I gave her all my candy.

Every day after that for a whole month, I kept pestering her about when the phone would arrive. She kept saying TOMORROW. But tomorrow never came. On top of that, I snuck out of my room late at night a couple times and spied her eating my candy while she watched Peacock News. She really TRICKED me good.

NOVEMBER

THURSDAY

When I went out to catch the school bus this morning, I discovered those teens in the electric car had pelted our house with cow manure and spray painted CARRION EATERS across the front door. Then I smelt the bacon Pops was frying in the kitchen and went back in to grab a few strips to go.

WEDNESDAY

Today in fifth period, I wished Ms. Copeland, our Phys Ed teacher, had told us that the boys were doing a wrestling unit for the next two months. That way I could do this whole bit about how the kids all thought she meant professional wrestling. But everybody knows that pro wrestling is not really a sport. It's carefully scripted and choreographed. Which means it's fake, like SOAP OPERA with PILEDRIVERS.

But if that really happened, some parent would probably sue the school for GENDER DISCRIMINATION, since giving the boys the exclusive opportunity to rub their bodies all over each other violated TITLE IX.

> No person in the United States shall, on the basis of sex, be excluded from participation in, be denied the benefits of, or be subjected to discrimination under any education program or activity receiving Federal financial assistance.

What really happened was that Ms. Copeland announced all students, boys and girls, were going to do a unit on BALLET. At first, I was disappointed because she told us that only the girls were allowed to wear TUTUS. By contrast, the boys had to put on these skin-tight leggings with bulbous CODPIECES to hide our privates.

I'm getting bored of dropping lazily rendered doodles here, so I'll force you to scrape your eyeballs over some classic art instead. High culture!

But at home that afternoon I BINGED (Mr. NOTE FENCES said he would pay me a hundred bucks for the product placement) "famous ballet dancers" and found the bio of this dude named MIKHAIL BARYSHNIKOV. Apparently, he defected to the US from this place called the SOVIET UNION, which I've never heard of, spends a lot of time in France, and recently became a citizen of LATVIA due to "extraordinary merits." When lots of countries are fighting over you, you must be super-popular. I bet the hot girls all LOVE him. So I'm all-in on ballet.

I'd make this joke now about how I'm having second thoughts about getting TOO GOOD at ballet because this kid in my school—who may or may not be AFRICAN-AMERICAN—won this award for being the best basketball player. Then, due to his newfound visibility, he got made fun of for having a funny-sounding name.

But that would show how AMBIVALENT I am about being popular. Do I want to hide out and get bullied for being a nobody? Or do I want to stand out and be mocked for being too successful? It's a tough choice.

Mr. Truby says I'm the most passive type of comic protagonist—the NERD. The nerd's high is clinging to the illusion that he's successful. His low is that he's actually incompetent, unattractive, and bumbling. The nerd's psychological needs are to gain confidence and overcome loneliness. He usually doesn't have much of a moral need, because he's so weak, he's the victim. But for the jokes to work, the nerd type has to think he's cool, otherwise there's no way to "drop" him, that is, make jokes at his expense.

Sometimes I wish I were a more active type of comic protagonist, like an everyman, know-it-all, showbiz type, princess, aristocrat, boor, trickster, or traveling angel.

But at least I think I'm cool, so we should be good.

THURSDAY

Today I found out that, to be fair, Ms. Copeland would let the boys wear TUTUS just like the girls. Otherwise, it would be GENDER DISCRIMINATION, and the school could get sued. The Principal was worried about the can of worms letting boys wear tutus would open. So he made Ms. Copeland switch our unit to SQUARE DANCING.

That's fine with me. It means I'll get to interact with REAL FEMALE GIRLS, which is a rare phenomenon in some other diaries you may have read. And I get to wear a COWBOY HAT and BOOTS, which is pretty much the same thing as a CODPIECE, if you think about it. Seriously, think about it.

The first thing Ms. Copeland did was to assign us partners. She paired me with Freckly. This made me very uncomfortable. There are some boys who dance with other boys at the school dances. But I'm too terrified to even ask a REAL FEMALE GIRL to dance.

I have to say, though, when Freckly put his hands on my hips and looked me in the eyes, I felt really SEEN. Maybe for the first time in my life.

TUESDAY

The GREAT BALLET CONTROVERSY, as the kids are calling it, has totally turned the school upside down. Now most of the boys are showing up wearing TUTUS. And the girls are all wearing CODPIECES.

At recess, hordes of them are fluttering around the four square court doing their PLIÉS and GRANDES JETÉS. Sometimes a couple will sneak off to the schoolyard gladiator pit to do their own special PAS DE DEUX.

I'm not sure what I have to do to become the Principal Dancer for the school ballet company. It may involve vaulting a lot higher during my TOUR EN L'AIR.

It's also making square dancing awkward with my partner Freckly. I have to figure out some way to switch partners. Normally, I'm so terrified of other people that I'm never actually WITH them. I'm in my head, scheming and worrying. But doing all that ballet at recess has lifted my sense of self-worth. So now things are getting a little too INTIMATE with Freckly.

TUESDAY

Actually, thanks to ballet, all the kids are getting along better than ever. Usually when kids talk to each other, it's not much of a conversation. They're either showing off or putting each other down or droning on about the trivial details of their sheltered lives and boring routines. Or worse, they're arguing about what game to play and what the rules are, then spending the whole time they're playing the game accusing each other of cheating.

But now they actually seem to respect each other. In conversation, the kids listen without interrupting each other. They ask follow-up questions that show that they were actually listening, not just rehearsing in their heads what they're going to say next. They acknowledge other kids' feelings. Exude a calm acceptance of the other's very BEING.

But I'm not ready to do any of that. I'm just a kid. Besides, most grownups are terrible at conversation too. And to be honest, all this harmony is kind of creepy. I feel more than ever like a cast-aside slice of moldy cheese.

My plan with Freckly is to be more MANLY. That way, he'll ask to be paired off with another square dance partner, because Freckly prefers to lead. And everyone knows that, in a duet, the more MANLY person always leads.

Now, as you know, the best way to be manly is to have lots of muscles. If I'm ripped, when Freckly grabs ahold of me during our square dances, he'll feel nothing but rock hard triceps. On top of that, in the upcoming BELLY DANCING unit in Phys Ed, I won't feel MORTIFIED about showing my scrawny, mushy pre-pubescent body.

They did some exotic stuff in the Orient back in the day.

That's one of so many great things about America. All the perfect bodies kids see in the media make them ashamed of their own imperfect ones. Then we spend the rest of our lives trying to change our bodies to match the ideal—usually by buying lots of products like exercise equipment and diet shakes.

So BODY SHAME is not only really good for the economy, it gives kids a strong motivation to improve themselves. And if you're really committed to improving yourself, your BODY DYSMORPHIA might lead to an EATING DISORDER, which is a great way to change your self-image really quickly.

64

That afternoon, I told my plan to Pops. He said I was misguided. The best way to be manly, he explained, was to have lots of opinions. Not only that, but you have to make sure that everybody knows about your opinions at all times. You have to convince them of how right you are and how wrong they are. Or even better, surround yourself with folks who agree with everything you say, so you can be sure you'll win every argument.

People also need to hear from you how things in the world REALLY work, as well as any random facts rattling around in your head at any given time.

And it's best to interrupt them when you do all this explaining. It shows that what you have to say is more important than the nonsense they're blathering on about.

That's how you can be really MANLY.

I countered, but Pops cut in. If anything, he said, having lots of muscles will HURT you, because then women and gay men will OBJECTIFY you. I was going to ask him what *objectify* means, but I didn't because I wasn't really listening. I was planning my next clever rebuttal. Also, I didn't want to appear stupid for not knowing what the word meant. And I don't want to have to do the tiny bit of work it takes to learn a new word.

Luckily, he explained anyway. He said it means they'll just see you as MAN-CANDY, which is a problem he's had to deal with all his life.

Usually, I do the exact opposite of what Pops wants me to do. It might be because, like I said earlier, I'm scared of him. Getting lots of muscles could be a way to get the upper hand, since now it would be ME threatening HIM with VIOLENCE and not the other way around.

To paraphrase the German sociologist MIN COBWEBER, just as the state lays claim to a monopoly on violence within its territorial boundaries, the father is the only person to wield the threat of violence within the home. Except when his son can kick his ass.

But then I thought, maybe he expects me to contradict him. If I do get super-ripped, I'd just be playing into his hand. So I could outfox him by doing the opposite of the opposite of what he said I should do. Which is to say, I decided to do exactly what he said he wanted me to do.

So I needed a way to fill my head up with a buttload of opinions. Preferably SECOND-HAND and CLICHÉD ones. I didn't want to actually have to think stuff through on my own.

Based on what I see from grownups, the quickest way to do that is to binge watch either Wolf News or Peacock News. I decided to watch BOTH on my folks' computer late at night. Now I can provoke an argument with anyone I meet by simply whipping out the opposite opinion of what they believe in.

But I need a sparring partner. Pops said that in any debate you should single out a PATSY to be your opponent. Patsies are guaranteed to spout off a lame version of the opposing argument. Or, if you can't find one, turn them into a STRAW MAN. To make a straw man, you simply PARAPHRASE whatever your opponent says into an oversimplified version. That makes it easy for you to knock him—and his argument—down.

I know the perfect patsy. After school I got Jowley to come over.

But Jowley refused to play along. When I said CLIMATE CHANGE IS A HOAX or GOVERNMENT IS EVIL, he said, "Interesting. Tell me more." So I tried a different approach. When I said, CAPITALISM IS EVIL or GOD DOESN'T EXIST, he just calmly replied, "Is that so?"

It's like Jowley has mastered some kind of intellectual JIU-JITSU. Just by him being genuinely curious, I start to doubt the validity of all my firmly-held beliefs. Friends are supposed to echo all your opinions. They're supposed to share the exact same point-of-view as you.

And if they can't be bothered to do that, they should at least have the common courtesy to roll over.

By that measure, Jowley's a lousy friend.

WEDNESDAY

Today in Geography, Ms. Diamond gave us a quiz. I usually look forward to quizzes in most classes, because they're really easy. All I have to do is cram the morning before by memorizing a bunch of facts. Then I REGURGITATE them on the quiz, score an A, and forget all about them the next day.

One day, when Mrs. Krabappel was feeling DISILLUSIONED about our school, she confessed that most teachers love quizzes too. She said it's an easy way for them to create the appearance that students are actually learning something, without doing much work. That's because it's easy to rip bits of information out of its LEARNING CONTEXT and shape it into multiple choice or fill-in-the-blank questions.

Plus, grading quizzes takes a lot less time than engaging your students in MEANINGFUL CONVERSATIONS about the subject they're studying. Overworked, underpaid teachers don't want to have to write thoughtful line-by-line responses to heap upon heap of poorly written essays.

She all but admitted that the education system conditions kids, by design, to chase grades. The powers-that-be prefer a docile population. One that's jerked around like pawns on the great chessboard of life by EXTRINSIC MOTIVATION.

So students come to LOVE activities like quizzes, which reward them with little GOLD STARS of so-called academic achievement, just like rats in an experiment getting a pellet of food for pressing a red button. Kids can then grow up, she said, to be obedient little knowledge workers in our post-industrial service economy.

Anyway, Mr. Diamond must be a GLUTTON FOR PUNISHMENT. Instead of quizzing us on the state capitals—a pointless but easy exercise in memorization and regurgitation—he asked us to read this thick book called *Columbus Was a Jerk Who Spread Cooties*.

Hey you over there, would you happen to have any pepper? No. How about gold? No? Then I'll settle for slaves.

It's about how the dominance of Western European civilization wasn't caused by racial and moral superiority, but rather, by an accident of geography. Then he asked us to write an essay about what we, as Americans, were personally going to do about all the peoples we've oppressed throughout our short, bloody history.

The Cow Pock _ or _ the Wonderful Effects of the New Inoculation!

A European "gift" for the natives of the "Americas."

Luckily, I figured out a way to avoid having to think too much about the topic. Which, you have to admit, is kind of depressing. I handed in a paper where I wrote, in so many words, NOT MUCH. In his comments, Mr. Diamond praised my essay's honesty and realism. He gave it a C+.

After he handed out all the papers, Mr. Diamond read out loud the essay of this annoying REAL FEMALE GIRL named Fatty Sterile. He said it was one of the best essays he'd read in his twenty years of teaching middle school geography. So much so, that it inspired him to quit his job and move to Tibet to become a monk.

I don't get why he thought it was so great. In it, Fatty just argued that the real driver of history wasn't the TRANSITORY ACCUMULATION OF EPISTEMIC POWER but the

COSMOLOGICAL DISSOLUTION OF ONTOLOGICAL IGNORANCE, rendering the whole point of *Columbus Was a Jerk Who Spread Cooties* moot.

I wasn't going to mention Fatty Sterile's essay here in my journal. My editor made me do it. She said I needed to give my character a pretext—however flimsy—for the act of violence I'm about to perpetrate on Fatty in the next chapter. No one likes a know-it-all.

THURSDAY

Mummy came into my room last night with a taser in her hand. That could only mean one thing. She was going to her KRAV MAGA class. Also, she mentioned that the school was holding tryouts for a school musical and that I should go.

Mummy forces me to do things I don't want to do all the time. She thinks that, as a parent, it's her job to expose me to the culture of those in higher social classes. That way, I might move up in the world. She'd also like to mold me into the kind of person she wishes she would've become had her own parents not been so lacking.

Usually, I love to do school musicals. Our music teacher, Ms. Farinelli, tells me all the time how lovely my SOPRANO voice is. I like to sing over all the other kids. She also said I have a tendency to be a DIVA.

Bonus points for figuring out who this is.

I was sure this year's school play was going to be *The Wizard of Oz*. It would be easy to do a supporting role like a singing tree. That way, I could do some slapstick gags and crack a few easy jokes about how I kept trying to cop out of even this tiny obligation.

What I was really worried about, though, was that Ms. Farinelli would assign me the role of the Cowardly Lion. Then I'd have to confront the uncomfortable similarities between that character and myself. I might even learn something.

But today I learned the school play was going to be DUDE ON THE TEN DOLLAR BILL. In solidarity with the FIRST

NATIONS PEOPLES OF NORTH AMERICA, I swore to
boycott TEN DOLLAR MAN. That's because, even though it's
supposed to be about the American Revolution, the musical lacks
even one indigenous character. Not only that, it doesn't even
MENTION Native Americans. Not once.

Rationally enlightened parvenue.

That would be like telling the story of the American Civil War while
failing to mention SLAVERY.

I explained all this to Pops, even interrupting him a few times
to hammer my point home. I got him to talk to Mummy about it.
Naturally, the TALK escalated into a FIGHT. But she won. She
always wins their fights. She said the need for me to CLIMB
SOCIALLY trumped any moral values I might have.

Pops would threaten Mummy with physical violence to get his way. But he can't, she says, because of this thing called the VIOLENCE AGAINST WOMEN ACT. Luckily for Pops, though, it's still legal in most states to use CORPORAL PUNISHMENT on your kids. Pops said if I didn't try out for the play, not only would they ground me, he'd also give me a SPANKING. He said it would be for my own good. To teach me self-discipline.

FRIDAY

A bunch of kids showed up to the tryout in character for the part they wanted. The boys wore long wool coats with lapels, knee-high breeches, a vest, a frilly linen shirt with lace cuffs, silk stockings showing off their calves, medium-heeled leather shoes, a powdered wig, a silk CRAVAT, and a tricorn hat.

The girls wore long silk gowns with a slim bodice on top and wide skirts on the bottom. To make their waists as trim as possible, they wore corsets under the bodice that were so tight they could hardly breath. Hoop petticoats under the skirt were stiffened by whale bone. On their heads, they wore their hair close and covered it with a white linen cap with lace lappets. The cap also had colorful silk streamers dangling from it.

Hubba hubba.

They ALL reeked of body odor masked by perfume. They were wearing dentures that made their teeth look all rotten. They sipped this nasty stuff called SHERRY and snorted this powder called SNUFF up their noses every two minutes. They had greasepaint slathered all over their faces. Some went so far as to apply these fake mole-like black spots to their cheeks called LUNAS. It was supposed to hide the sores they got from SYPHILIS.

Look closely. Can you spot the venereal disease?

It made me feel really cheap in my t-shirt, shorts, and sneakers—all imported from sweatshops in Bangladesh.

Ms. Farinelli had everyone perform "Fight the Power" by Public Enemy to test our rapping skills. I did my best to mumble the lyrics, especially the parts about Elvis and John Wayne, because I have too much respect for them to say such mean things about them.

If you don't know who those guys were, Elvis invented Rock n' Roll, and John Wayne was this cowboy who became President in 1980 and warned all the INNER CITY KIDS to JUST SAY NO or else he'd toss them in PRISON.

John Wayne's wife trickling down to the strapping young bucks cashing in
food stamps for T-bone steaks.

Of course, I got singled out, as usual. You'd think I'd want to be singled-out, because that's what it means to be popular. But I only want to stand out for the things I think are cool, like WINNING ARGUMENTS and doing the best GRANDE JETÉ. Otherwise, I'd prefer to blend into the crowd, if you don't mind.

Ms. Farinelli said I'd make a great HYPE MAN. That way I can stand out, but not too much. She said that TEN DOLLAR MAN was a great hype man for ONE BUCK GEEZER, so maybe I should play the lead. I nearly pooped my pants right then and there. Luckily, only a little came out. One more racing strip to add to the collection in my TIGHTY-WHITEYS.

But then Fatty Sterile tried out for the lead. Her rapping was better than everyone's by a long shot. She said it's because she grew up singing along to NWA CDs.

Pops once told me you should keep track of all the slights you think people have done to you then always be scheming about how to get back at them. He says it's the best way to give your life meaning, besides having a baby when you're a teenager. Since hearing that, I've made it a point of pride to be the top kid in my school at holding a grudge.

Jowley told me I should try out to play this guy who was the THIRD VICE PRESIDENT. Ten Dollar Man said something mean about him at a dinner party once. A gentleman's reputation is everything. So Third Vice President shot Ten Dollar Man in a duel. I'd love to shoot Fatty Sterile in a duel. I could sneak real black powder and lead shot into the stage prop flintlock pistol. Or would that be going too far?

Ms. Farinelli showed us a pirated copy of the musical. I fell asleep for half of it and dreamt of the SHAWNEE CHIEF TECUMSAH and HIS dream of a FEDERATION of Native American tribes that would expel the pale-faced invaders once and for all.

If only I could convince them to go home.

But I woke up just in time to figure out what role I should try out for—Ten Dollar Man's love interest. He cheats on her but she sticks around anyway. Not because wives were essentially men's property back then, but because, like me, she was really vindictive. She realized the best way to get revenge on Ten Dollar Man was for her to author how people remembered him. She could fill his public legacy up with all sorts of distortions that fool future generations into thinking HISTORY is made by the GRAND ACTS of HEROIC MEN.

> Universal History, the history of what man has accomplished in this world, is at bottom the History of the Great Men who have worked here. They were the leaders of men, these great ones; the modellers, patterns, and in a wide sense creators, of whatsoever the general mass of men contrived to do or to attain; all things that we see standing accomplished in the world are properly the outer material result, the practical realization and embodiment, of Thoughts that dwelt in the Great Men sent into the world: the soul of the whole world's history, it may justly be considered, were the history of these.
>
> —Some Old British Git

And I can do the same for dearest Fatty Sterile. Who I DON'T have a crush on. I swear.

Luckily for me, none of the girls tried out for the part. They were all too sore from having to wear those brutal corsets.

WEDNESDAY

I'm getting used to the hoop skirts by wearing my costume around the house. I've knocked over a few lamps and picture frames, but I'm getting the hang of it. I love to curtsy.

After school, I CAJOLE—because that's how ladies got their way back then—Cowlick, Jowley, Fanny, Pops, and Mummy into practicing a few CONTREDANCES FRANCAISES with me. Cowlick is an oaf. He's always stepping on my skirts. But we're making good progress.

FRIDAY

There's a rule at school that everybody who tries out for a play has to get a part. The school wants to mislead kids into thinking there's a place for everyone in TOURNAMENT PROFESSIONS like actor, athlete, pop singer, or college professor. That way, more young adults will throw away their most productive years chasing the PIPE DREAM of making it BIG ONE DAY. A larger pool of talent means better quality at the top. The winners get to be famous multi-millionaires while the rest wait tables, get buried in debt, and sink into mental illness.

So now Ms. Farinelli has to make up extra parts for all the kids who tried out. Luckily for them, most of society back then consisted of illiterate peasants, indentured servants, and slaves.

This one lucky kid who tried out to be One Buck Geezer got to be a Scots-Irish immigrant under indenture to One Buck Geezer. During the play, he held the transit that One Buck Geezer used to survey the lands his fellow ANGLOS were planning to steal from the natives. But if he ever dropped the transit and broke it, One Buck Geezer would give him twenty lashes, because the instrument was worth more than he was.

This land is now OUR land.

The surplus girls got to realize their creative potential by serving as a chorus of spinners, seamstresses, milliners, washerwomen, milkmaids, wet nurses, nannies, and midwives. A few lucky ones got to sit around and be pregnant for the whole musical.

I really envy most the kids who got to play slaves, though. Their benevolent masters, like DUDE ON THE TWO DOLLAR BILL, took really good care of them. They were given warm clothes, shelter, and got fed every day. If they'd been free, they definitely would've been worse off.

DECEMBER

THURSDAY

The play is only a few days from now, but I'm worried it's going to be TOO GOOD. All the kids with major roles have gone totally METHOD. They prance around the halls between classes in costume and even talk like they did back in the eighteenth-century, spouting off all these THYs and THOUs, highfalutin vocab, and complicated syntax. They even tried to get the Principal to make the school mascot a HARLOT or a RAKE.

The problem is they all know their lines so well, the show risks being too ROBOTIC. There's no room for playful IMPROVISATION or any beautiful OOPS.

Yesterday, Ms. Farinelli brought in her pet amoeba to play King George III. But when PEOPLE FOR THE ETHICAL TREATMENT OF ANIMALS found out, they filed a complaint with the county. They said it was too degrading for even a single-celled organism to be forced to play an INBRED ARISTOCRAT who was not only a parasite on the body politic, but a war-mongering sociopath to boot.

I'm fancy.

At this point, you're probably wondering why I've been yammering on about this school play for a dozen pages, when Jowley isn't even in it. The episode doesn't really move the plot forward, apart from giving me the chance to show, once again, how all my selfish schemes are dashed to bits by ironic twists of fate.

What can I say? I'm a kid. I like stories that go AND THEN, AND THEN, AND THEN.

TUESDAY

Tonight was the premier of the school play. For some reason, Ms. Farinelli renamed it to *Dude on the Ten Dollar Bill Who Should Be Replaced By That Old Lady Who Ran the Underground Railroad But White Supremacists In Power Won't Let That Happen.* I was really happy to see from the stage that my whole family came, including Cowlick.

Postponed again. Really?

He even got into the spirit of the age by wearing his clip-on tie. It's a little inside joke we share. As I'm sure you already know, the modern neck-tie's earliest ancestor was the CRAVAT. In the seventeenth-century, the King of France, Louis XIV, invented the cravat when he saw how dandy the Croatian mercenaries he'd hired to wage war looked with their traditional bright kerchiefs knotted around their manly necks.

I'm too sexy for my cravat.

So whenever Cowlick wears his clip-on tie, he's signaling to me that I should feel like a KING. He even promised to record a video of the performance on his smartphone and post it to WatchMePleaseImBeggingYouTube for all his friends-of-expediency to enjoy.

He said there's a good chance it may even go VIRAL. Not in a bad way like COVID-19, but in a good way like #METOO.

Art or porn? #METOO

I could tell you about how the play was a total disaster—just one fiasco after another. But I don't think it's very nice to turn off so many impressionable minds to theater.

Actually, the performance was MEDIOCRE, as you'd pretty much expect from a bunch of middle schoolers. But we had fun. That was the important thing.

Or, at least, that's what grownups seem to think is important for kids our age. It's not really until high school when they start measuring us against adult standards of excellence. Until then, they seem pretty content to heap easy praise on every little thing we do, no matter how crappy. Which suits my fragile self-esteem just fine.

Also, the thing I love most about theater is that when I get into character, I'm no longer me. So I don't feel that constant embarrassment. Whatever the audience thinks of me doesn't really matter, because, for those precious few hours, I'm free of all my nagging insecurities.

Even Fanny didn't recognize me up there as Ten Dollar Man's wife. When I came on stage, he yelled out, "Pretty!"

I guess, though, for some perverse reason, I actually LIKE to put myself in embarrassing situations. Maybe it's my subconscious trying to find ways to give me the chance to GET OVER MYSELF and start living.

Am I the seer or what I see?

I'd tell you I got revenge on Fatty Sterile and ruined the play. But I don't believe that just because a person objects strongly to something I do gives me the right to retaliate with physical violence. Besides, like I said earlier, my revenge was more subtle. I'm telling the story, which means what I say happened is what happened. Right?

SUNDAY

Christmas is a week away. I'd tell you I was too busy with school to think about Christmas until now, but you definitely wouldn't believe me. Every kid obsesses about Christmas pretty much as soon as the last bites of Thanksgiving pumpkin pie make their incredible journey through the human digestive tract and land with a plop in the magical portal to the municipal sewer system.

I'm excited about Christmas every year because it's a special time to celebrate the birth of Our Savior, the Lord Jesus Christ. We can rejoice knowing that Christ's SACRIFICE on the CROSS assures us all ETERNAL LIFE. I really look forward to attending Mass.

What did you get me, Santa?

Just kidding. I'm a patriot, not some religious freak. I love Christmas because it stimulates MAMMON, even more so than Halloween. Retail sales spike. Jobs are created. Profits are made. All this CONSUMERISM really warms the spirit.

Just kidding. I'm a kid, not a mealy-mouthed politician. I love Christmas because I get stuff without having to work for it. And like most kids, I've learned how to be strategic about what I ask for on my WISH LIST. I make a point of only asking for the stuff advertised to me during cartoon shows or for merchandise with promotional tie-ins to blockbuster movies.

Luckily for me, mainstream toys are rigidly gendered—think BOY BLUE, GIRL PINK—so it's hard to make the terrible mistake of wanting something that might muddle GENDER STEREOTYPES.

The great thing about my family is that Mummy is always browbeating Pops into making sure we don't buy into all that nonsense. At bedtime, Mummy reads me excerpts from GENDER TROUBLE by this lady named Judith Butler. She says gender roles are a kind of PERFORMANCE that has little to do with biology.

> As a result, gender is not to culture as sex is to nature; gender is also the discursive/cultural means by which 'sexed nature' or 'a natural sex' is produced and established as 'prediscursive,' prior to culture, a politically neutral surface on which culture acts.
>
> —Judith Butler

And to be sure we don't even make the mistake of thinking BIOLOGICAL SEX is simply male and female, Mummy likes to read to us from this book called *Biological Exuberance*. It's an exhaustive catalog of the diverse kinds of mating observed to occur in nature.

Two male Mallard ducks caught being unnatural.

Our science teacher, Ms. Kropotkin, has this pet theory that HOMOSEXUALITY and other expressions of SEX AMBIGUITY are a necessary EVOLUTIONARY ADAPTATION to our current environment.

One time when I was little I wanted a BARBIE doll house. Pops wouldn't get it for me, because he said it was inappropriate for boys. Mummy agreed, but for a different reason. She said it reinforced ANTIQUATED ideas of the FEMININE.

But I have a fallback when it comes to Christmas. My relatives are lazy and just give me cash. That way, I can buy whatever I want. I ordered the Barbie doll house online. What can I say. I like to ROLE PLAY with unrealistically proportioned blondes.

When you think about it, gift giving at Christmas is weird. I guess it's some sort of social lubricant. We have such a hard time showing our appreciation for the people in our lives.

We say thank you all the time. But because we say it so frequently, it becomes hollow. Or like when an acquaintance asks, "How are you?" and you say, "Great." You know they don't really want to know how you're TRULY feeling. If you answered honestly, by saying, for example, "TERRIFIED," you both make yourself vulnerable. You risk actually getting to know each other in a more intimate way. And that would be super-uncomfortable.

Christmas is like that. We take each other for granted for the rest of the year. But on Christmas we show our appreciation by buying each other stuff we don't really need and—let's be honest— don't even want.

Sure, us kids might say we really want some toy or other. And when we get it for Christmas, we might even get excited for a nanosecond. But, inevitably, we play with that shiny new toy for a little while, get bored, then start fixating on the next must-have merchandise being sold to us on TV.

But like I said, it's great for the economy. And that's definitely what Jesus wants for us—economic growth above all else.

THURSDAY

Speaking of Jesus, every year Mummy looks for some token way to feel less guilty about all the ABUNDANCE our family takes for granted while a lot of people in our community are POOR and ALONE.

Pops doesn't agree with her. He says being poor is their own fault. They need to pull themselves up by their own bootstraps.

If Mummy was really serious about helping the less fortunate, she should TITHE her income and donate it to the EVANGELICAL MEGACHURCH down the street from us. The pastor there preaches the Gospel Of Prosperity, which means you can have your cake and eat it too. He drives around in a MERCEDES, just like JESUS, so he must know what he's talking about.

So this is what Joshua ben Joseph really hand in mind.

He says that if you give 10% of your income to his church, you'll get it back a HUNDREDFOLD through mysterious ways. That sounds like a great return on your investment. If you loan your money to the federal government, all you get back these days is a couple pennies on the dollar.

But, no, Mummy insists on visiting old folks in the HOSPICE and offering to them something she should save only for her kids. I'm talking about UNCONDITIONAL LOVE.

Old people scare me. They're all shriveled and crusty. They smell bad. And wheeze a lot. But the thing about them that scares me the most is that weird glint they sometimes get in their eye. It's as if FACING DEATH brings INNER PEACE.

CHRISTMAS

I like to do things a little differently on Christmas. I don't want to be a ME ME ME clichÈ. I don't wake up at 6 am like most kids and immediately jump on my parents' bed and start pestering them about when I can rip open my presents.

Instead, I get up at 4 am. First, I pray for an hour or so, giving thanks for all the blessings in my life. Then I clean the house, as quietly yet thoroughly as I can. Next, I prepare a nice breakfast for my loving parents. Finally, I get dressed in my Sunday best and wait patiently on the couch, flogging myself with a cat-o-nine-tails, for the rest of the household to stir.

This year I was really excited to see Fanny open his presents and get everything he asked for. I was grateful to get several interesting books and a dozen pairs of socks, which I really needed, since many of my socks are crusty, if you know what I mean.

I didn't get anything for Cowlick. We have a brotherly agreement that, instead of exchanging gifts, we give each other the gift of our mutual companionship. Every winter month, we make a DATE where we do something together, like volunteer to pick up litter from the freeway or visit the children in the cancer ward at the local hospital.

I don't buy anything for my folks, either. I prefer to give them each a long, hand-written letter in my best cursive detailing how much I appreciate all the things they do for me without even expecting anything in return.

The best thing about this Christmas, though, was what my Uncle Gnarly got me. A fat stack of KITE WITH A KEY TIED TO IT GUY bills. I can't decide how to spend it all. I'm torn between investing it in T-BILLS or donating it to MEGACHURCH JESUS.

Pops surprised me later with a special gift he'd been saving. It was a brand new CODPIECE for ballet! I didn't have the heart to tell him I've moved on, in my never ending quest for a higher social station, to DRESSAGE.

Look, Mummy, I've arrived!

By the way, that's called a REINCORPORATION. It's when, in a comedy routine, you bring back something you mentioned a bit earlier, much to your audience's surprise and delight.

After all the festivities, I went over to Jowley's house to share glad tidings of the COMING OF OUR LORD and give him a present. I forget they're Jewish. Luckily for me, Hanukkah happened to fall around the same time as Christmas this year, so it was no big deal.

It's funny how so many of these kinds of holidays, no matter the tradition, happen around Winter Solstice. I guess we're all PAGANS at heart.

Opfer römischer Jungfrauen.

That looks like fun.

You're probably happy to read about Jowley again, aren't you?
I mean, for how long can I keep you interested by showing you
what a sneaky twerp I am and how all my schemes fail in surprising
ways? At its core, this is a buddy romance, more than a coming-of-
age tale, right? So where's the buddy been all this time?

Well, you should be happy to know that my friendship—if you can
call it that—with Jowley takes center stage for the rest of the
way.

Do you notice how, in the illustrations that accompany the older version of my tale, I'm always frowning? That's because I'm sad. Can you guess why I'm sad? By now, I should hope so.

Anyway, I forgot to buy Jowley a present. So I improvised. I got an industrial strength garbage bag and stuffed it with a bunch of the toilet paper, hand sanitizer, and N95 masks Pops was hoarding in the garage, plus a heap of old clothes that don't fit me and Cowlick anymore.

Did I mention that sometimes I find Mummy in the garage rubbing our old clothes all over her face and sobbing, "Where did I go wrong?"

Then I stuck one of those big sticky bows on the bag. It was like Santa's sack!

Jowley was so excited to root around in the sack. He said how thoughtful the gift was. Up until then, due to the TP shortage, he'd been using shreds of old t-shirts to wipe himself. They clogged up the sewer system, and his dad had to call the city workers. And how he loved the gently used BRIEFS the most. His mom makes him wear BOXERS, but he says he knows deep down he's a BRIEFS kind of guy.

But then he looked at the label and saw that the underwear was 50% cotton and 50% wool. He said his mom keeps the house strictly KOSHER and that the TORAH forbids mixing cotton and wool, which is called SHATNEZ. But he said, again, it's the thought that counts.

Then he pulled out his gift for me. Jowley's mom is a multi-billionaire, so I knew it was going to be good. It was a gift certificate from WOLF NEWS for 100 million dollars worth of advertising. Jowley said if I ever wanted to run for President, it would come in handy.

But that's not all. He got me a YOWAMUSHI brand ATV. But it's electric. I only like vehicles with COMBUSTION engines that guzzle gas and spew CARBON into the atmosphere. There's just nothing like burning FOSSIL FUELS to get your heart racing. But I tried my best to act grateful.

I'd like to make a joke about how kids getting things they didn't expect but want is a CHRISTMAS MIRACLE. But that would be too CRASS. Miracles are supposed to be about serious stuff like cures for cancer or orphaned twins finding each other. Not entitled BRATS getting yet more CRAP they don't need.

NEW YEAR'S EVE

In case you're wondering what I'm doing in the ER waiting room at 11:59 pm on New Year's Eve, let me enlighten you.

Earlier this evening, I was messing around with Fanny in the laundry room. Usually, I like to stuff him in the dryer and put it on LOW for five minutes. He gets nice and dizzy. When he starts to squeal, I let him out. But only after he begs for mercy.

You're probably not surprised because you know how SADISTIC boys can be. It's only for lack of imagination they don't KILL each other.

Also, what were my parent's thinking? Siblings tearing into each other is pretty much inevitable when you coop them up in a house together for an entire winter break, let alone for the duration of a pandemic.

But the trouble really started when I swiped Mummy's car keys, took them down to the Big Box Hardware Store and convinced a couple of veterans there, who were suffering from PTSD from all the illegal wars they'd been forced to wage as kids, to make me a copy.

I told Fanny that the plastic car he pushes around the house saying "vroom, vroom" was for babies. If he really wanted to be a BIG KID he needed to learn how to DUI. That's fancy grown-up code for driving back from the pub while acting totally normal.

I gave him a can of the sugary cocktail drink Pops keeps stashed away in his "private" fridge in the garage. Then I handed him the keys and invited him to drive me to Madagascar. He steered while I pushed the pedals. We made it out of the driveway, down the street, and onto the freeway.

I just got a scuff on my knee. But since Fanny is so little, the airbag didn't work so well on him. He needs to have a few vertebrae fused. Also, he's going to need brain surgery.

So here I am in the ER waiting room watching the BALL DROP on the TV bolted to the wall. And that's why my New Year's resolution is to never play with Fanny again.

JANUARY

WEDNESDAY

I found a way to make good use of the ATV Jowley got me for Christmas. I came up with this game where Jowley does DONUTS on the local golf course while I take pot-shots at the FUEL TANK with his mom's vintage WORLD WAR II LUGER pistol. His mom says she keeps it around to remind her of what kind of world we live in. My brilliant idea is to get the tank to explode. Jowley will be repelled by the fireball off the back of his seat. It will all look really cool, like in a MICHAEL BAY ACTION MOVIE.

It's a lot harder to hit a moving target than it is in video games. Plus the Luger tends to jam. It even backfired once and blew off my pinkie. Every shot I took missed the ATV and flew harmlessly into this crowd of TEENAGERS loitering outside the HIGH SCHOOL across the street.

They totally overreacted, though, and started PULLING THEIR HAIR OUT. The school admin even triggered the ACTIVE SHOOTER protocol. Sirens started blaring everywhere, while someone shouted RUN! HIDE! FIGHT! over the loudspeakers.

We ignored all the ruckus. But Jowley was being annoying. He kept begging me to have a turn with the Luger. I said it was too dangerous for him, because he hadn't played enough FIRST-

PERSON SHOOTER video games like I had. I was practically an expert with all types of firearms.

Good guys with guns stop bad guys with guns.

I ran out of bullets before I could hit the target. But at least the game keeps me out of the house. It's INSUFFERABLE to spend even a second in there. My folks always spoil Fanny. But now, since his "episode," they treat him like a MAD PRINCE. He's already figured out that anything he wants, he gets. All he has to do is start acting all twitchy and Mummy's right at his side kissing up to him. Disgusting.

THURSDAY

I was going over to Jowley's house today. My plan was to convince him to sneak into his mom's workshop and make some more bullets. But Mummy said I had to finish my thank-you cards for all the loot I got from relatives at Christmas.

I never like it when Mummy forces me to say THANK YOU or make a big show of being GRATEFUL. She says I'd be happier if I made a list every day of all the things I was grateful for in life. Fake it until you feel it. That's her motto.

Call me crazy, though, but I think GRATITUDE should arise spontaneously out of an overall feeling of WELL-BEING. It shouldn't be this contrived thing I force myself to do just because I should.

I was going to share with you this little bit where I came up with this elaborate scheme to turn my thank-you note writing into a fill-in-the-blank form letter. That way you could see I'm not lazy. I'll make a lot of effort to scam somebody. But then the scheme backfires in a silly MAD LIBS way, because you can't cookie-cut GRATITUDE.

But I think you can. I'd say 90% of daily American social interaction could be boiled down to a single, resoundingly insincere THANK YOU.

Anyway, the relatives sent me cash, so I figure the most I owe them is a text message with a string of EMOJIS.

That pretty much says all I need to say.

FRIDAY

I still couldn't hit the gas tank on the ATV. But I managed to pop Jowley in the left eye. I figured he'd just wipe off the blood with his sleeve and get back on the ATV. But he just laid there all curled up like a baby.

I tried to make him laugh, but all the usual jokes didn't work. So I knew he was going to be a wimp about it.

MONDAY

Finally, we're back at school. Of course, Jowley was such a sore loser. He wouldn't stop reminding me about the ATV accident. He didn't even have to say anything. It was right there, written on his smug face. 'Cause he was wearing this big black eye patch.

The worst part of it is that now all the other kids are giving Jowley attention I should be getting. They keep saying—right to my face—that he's cooler than I am because he looks like a real pirate.

I can't believe Jowley's more popular than me now. He was supposed to be the sidekick, not the other way around.

A gaggle of HOT GIRLS even invited him to join them for lunch. They asked him if they could peek under the patch. And he let them! I just don't get it. It's just an empty eye socket, all craggy with dried blood. They swoon and tell him it's REVOLTING, but in a really EROTIC way.

What annoys me is that he still has ONE GOOD EYE. It's not like he's BLIND or anything. Sure, he doesn't have depth perception any more, so he keeps walking into walls and stabbing the desk with his pen and getting these terrible migraine headaches. But he can still see just fine, thank you very much.

TUESDAY

I'm seeing now how Jowley's "handicap," if you'll let me call it that, is such a great scam. One I'd like to get in on. But I thought I'd do him one better.

So I used our backyard grill to heat up the iron poker from the fireplace until its tip was glowing orange. Then I gouged out BOTH my eyes.

I thought now all the HOT GIRLS would totally want to take care of me. They'd lead me around school, feed me, and help me take baths and get dressed. It'd be heaven on earth.

But when I got to school this morning, I discovered something. Everybody thinks blind people are CREEPY. Unless you can sing SOUL MUSIC. My soprano voice is more suited to CHANSON. So the hot girls want nothing to do with me. They wouldn't even let me grope their faces so I could GET TO KNOW them.

Freckly said I could feel his face, if I wanted. He said he knew SIGN LANGUAGE. But I said that was for DEAF PEOPLE.

Awkward. I told him if he really wanted to show empathy he should learn BRAILLE.

Geez. Why do kids always lump the DIFFERENTLY ABLED into one CATEGORY and insult them by giving their label for them a CONDESCENDINGLY POSITIVE SPIN?

MONDAY

Last week, the second semester started, so now I have all new classes. I signed up for these really useful subjects: BURGER FLIPPING, ADVANCED PEER PRESSURE, SKIN CARE, and my favorite, TEEN PARENTING SKILLS.

I also wanted to sign up for SHOP 2, but I was afraid everyone at school would make fun of me for being so WORKING CLASS. I've tried to explain to them that many carpenters, plumbers, and electricians make this thing called PREVAILING WAGE, which affords them a solid middle-class lifestyle.

But they always scoff and say if you're not a KNOWLEDGE WORKER, you're a PROLE. I counter by insisting I'd rather have a job where I make real stuff. Besides, most office jobs involve a lot of BUSYWORK that serves no purpose besides greasing the BUREAUCRATIC machinery. I'd rather grease actual machinery.

But being good at HVAC doesn't exactly move you up the pecking order at school. Which, if you think about it, is great training for an office job, since students also do a lot of pointless busywork.

Anyway, instead of SHOP 2, I enrolled in Dependency Studies. The idea is that the class surveys all the ways their parents act like machines. Then we're supposed to come up with a plan to help free them from their programming.

The catch is that there isn't a grade. At the end of the course, the teacher assesses the quality and overall effectiveness of our INTERVENTION. Basically, the more effectively we can get our parents to break a bad habit, the better we do.

I'm not all that optimistic about the team I was assigned to. I found out that the teacher assigned ME to my own team. If I'm no more than a bunch of UNCONSCIOUS CONDITIONING, how can I expect to liberate anyone else from the same plight, especially my parents?

TUESDAY

On the first day of class our team made a list on the whiteboard of all the things the grownups we know are addicted to. Here's what we came up with:

Coffee, sugar, arguing, alcohol, serial dating, sex, prescription drugs, illegal drugs, smartphones, social media, eating dead animal flesh, fossil fuels, horse race politics, gambling, thinking, exercise, work, careerism, porn, judging, analyzing, having opinions, smoking, procrastination, cynicism, positivity, diet soda, processed foods, the internet, video games, television, the news, gossip, militarism, tardiness, pulp fiction, trivia, nostalgia, get-rich-quick schemes, busyness, interrupting, stereotypes, doubt, complaining, the future, the past, makeup, fashion, pleasure, pain, suffering, the self, picking their nose, popping zits, money, fad diets, naturopathic remedies, righteous indignation, arguing, resentment, shopping, debt, hoarding, New Age mysticism, religious dogma, cultural identity, gendering, nationalism, sleeping, despair, autoerotic asphyxiation, fun

When we reviewed the list, everybody kind of freaked out. We thought it'd be impossible to choose even one of these things, let alone get our parents to quit doing it.

But Mr. Banks told us the best way to get someone to change was to lead by example. This means doing two things. First, we make a sincere effort to observe our own conditioning. By being curious about our own habits, we open ourselves to the possibility of an insight into the root causes of them. With insight and loving acceptance, habits dissolve naturally without us having to exercise willpower. Second, we don't need to change anybody. People in our lives will notice the transformation within us and some will, as a consequence, become curious about their own conditioning.

Now, as you know, I'm lazy. I don't like doing much for myself—like homework, making breakfast, or brushing my teeth. Also, I tend to think of girls as only being interested in dating and makeup. Also, that girls only like to talk, while boys take action. Mr. Banks suggested I get sincerely curious about why that is.

Turning inward makes me really uncomfortable, though. I'm afraid I may not like what I find in there. Mr. Banks says that's me being hard on myself. Just obverse, he said. Observe with loving acceptance what arises within.

While Mr. Banks was saying all this, I noticed he had his finger jammed halfway up his nostril. I pointed that out to him. He blushed and said Dependency Studies was cancelled.

THURSDAY

We had a general assembly in school this morning. Usually at this time every year, they show us a movie called INTERSECTIONALITY. It's about how we all tend to lump people into stereotypes based on their race, class, and gender. We have unexamined biases about these categories, which often lead to discrimination.

Pops says that's all just POLITICALLY CORRECT whining by a bunch of mooching snowflakes who hide behind collective grievances, rather than assert themselves as free-thinking individuals. Mummy says it's self-serving for Pops to think that, because he's a WHITE MALE.

But this year, they showed us a new movie called, YOU ARE NOT AN OBJECT. It talked about how your TRUE SELF isn't something that can be named or known as an object. It's that which OBSERVES all objects—a PURE SUBJECT that transcends all IDENTITIES, whether racial, class-based, gendered, or personal. Knowing yourself as the True Self is the only way to enjoy lasting peace and freedom.

I got really confused.

The movie went on to really blow my mind. They interviewed this lady who said WESTERN CULTURE has a worldview that's BACKWARDS. Most of us believe that first there's MATTER, then LIFE, then HUMAN BRAINS, then INDIVIDUAL CONSCIOUSNESS. But, she said, if we observe carefully, there's no actual evidence of this.

In fact, it's the other way around. First comes universal consciousness then material objects that arise within and from it, like subatomic particles, stars, planets, living bodies, and human brains. Fundamentally, our individual person is an expression of UNIVERSAL CONSCIOUSNESS.

How did life get so complicated?

So who am I REALLY? The intersection of a bunch of labels or universal consciousness? And how do I find out?

Later on, they made an announcement about a few openings on the Secret Intelligence Service Student Corps, or as the kids like to call it, SISSY. Their job is to protect school leaders and make sure they stay in power, no matter how unjust they happen to be.

Pops always says the best way to be happy is by being popular. The best way to be popular is by having power. And the best way to gain power is by sowing FEAR.

I needed an escape from all the self-doubt swirling around in my skull after watching that disturbing movie. SISSY sounded like the perfect escape. And I always love a chance to abuse whatever authority anyone is foolish enough to give me.

I went down to Mr. Naryshkin's basement office and asked to sign up. I got Jowley to go with me. Mr. Naryshkin asked us if we were familiar with the latest WATERBOARDING techniques. That's a sport where you use a small foam board to surf the waves. We don't live by the coast, but I figured, how hard could it be? So I said, yeah, sure.

Mr. Naryshkin issued us our badges. He said we should hide them in one of our ORIFICES and only take them out when we absolutely needed to. I guessed ORIFICE was just a fancy word for

POCKET. The rest of the time we should just blend it. It's the SECRET service after all, he chuckled.

That sucks. The whole point of joining SISSY was to use it to LORD it over my classmates.

Then Mr. Naryshkin gave us our first job. He said some of the eighth-graders were spreading FAKE NEWS to get the Principal fired. Our mission was to INFILTRATE the most popular eighth-grade cliques, find out who was saying those mean things, then report back to him with their names.

We should consider it a probationary assignment. If it went well, he promised to put us in charge of the school's EXTRAORDINARY RENDITION program.

To complete our mission, we'd have to hang out with the eighth-graders in the hallways during their lunch period. I realized that meant we'd miss twenty minutes of ETHICS & DEMOCRACY class.

Jowley must have figured that out too, because he started to protest. Mr. Naryshkin's eyes narrowed. He said that the first rule of SISSY was BLIND OBEDIENCE. It was not our place to question the WISDOM of our superiors. If we did, we may find out it's us being WATERBOARDED. Jowley is afraid of the ocean, so that shut him up real fast. Since I'm already blind, I'm halfway there.

I couldn't believe my good fortune. Now I had the power to ruin the life of any eighth-grader I didn't like.

TUESDAY

Today was the first day of our SISSY mission. Me and Jowley technically don't have a territory like the Crossing Guards or the Hall Monitors. But that didn't stop us from making our own rounds just before homeroom. Flashing our badges, we shook down the kids we came across for their lunch money, saying it was INSURANCE in case anything BAD might happen to them. We also offered them Bathroom Passes for five bucks each. For only the first day, we made quite a haul.

Another great perk of SISSY is you get to roll into first period half an hour late. You pick any seat you like, and if there's a kid already sitting there, they have to move. Also, during class, the kids around you have to do your work for you AND polish your sneakers. When it's time to take a quiz or test, they have to give you all the answers. And if you get anything less than a 95%, you get to DISAPPEAR them as punishment.

I'm telling you, I've got it made with this SISSY gig.

At 11 am, me and Jowley ditched our Ethics & Democracy class to go hang out with the eighth-graders. To make it easier to earn their trust, Mr. Naryshkin gave us some VAPE PENS and ADDERALL to hand out. Apparently, that's what teens are into these days. Still, they were reluctant to open up to us, because we were PREPUBESCENT TWERPS, after all.

But then I had an idea. Everybody is desperate to feel close to celebrities. So I told them my uncle was the pop star SEAMSTRESS SPEEDY's bodyguard. Suddenly, I was their best friend.

FEBRUARY

WEDNESDAY

Today we had our fifth big PANDEMIC of the year, so they canceled school again. One of the things I love about GLOBALIZATION is how small it makes the world. Now when some disease starts in, say, Asia, because everything is so interconnected, it spreads quickly to the rest of the world.

Pops complains that even though ALCOHOLISM, CAR CRASHES, HEART ATTACKS, and SEASONAL FLU kill way more people every year than the latest pandemic, the MEDIA can't resist whipping up a PANIC, because it increases their RATINGS. So everybody totally freaks out. I don't mind, though, 'cause it means we kids don't have to go to school or learn anything.

Mummy hates it because she thinks of school as free daycare. On SHELTER-IN-PLACE days, she puts Cowlick in charge of me and Fanny. That usually doesn't work out so well, because Cowlick tries to lead by CONSENSUS rather than FEAR, so we don't respect his authority and do whatever we want.

Usually, I like to hang out by myself on days off like this. That's because, as I said, I'm a MISANTHROPE, so I find SOCIAL DISTANCING easy.

But today, I texted Jowley and told him to get his butt over to my house. Me and him have been trying to figure out a cheap way to reverse GLOBAL WARMING.

Jowley says we should invent a machine that SEQUESTERS CARBON DIOXIDE from the atmosphere. But I don't like that idea. I think it'll give folks a free pass to keep burning fossil fuels, which have lots of other bad side effects besides CO_2 emissions.

I want us to invent a contraption that gets microbes to produce edible PROTEIN cheaply through FERMENTATION. That way, we won't chop down so many forests to grow food for our livestock. But Jowley says people will never want to eat double-cheeseburgers made from bacteria farts. I counter that grownups already drink YEAST POOP. It's called vodka.

We go back and forth and never get anywhere. But today we finally settled on an idea we both like. We're going to build in my garage a FUSION REACTOR. Cheap, plentiful energy that will absolutely wipe out the fossil fuel industry.

All we have to do is get our hands on some DEUTERIUM, then come up with a cool way to squeeze it down into a superhot PLASMA.

First, we stripped a quartz tube from an old TV. Next, we duct-taped a bunch of fridge magnets around the tube, then wrapped copper wires around the magnets. When it was done, we jammed the whole setup into the dryer cylinder and wired it into the electrical.

Now all we had to do was get ahold of some DEUTERIUM. We called the local NUCLEAR POWER PLANT to ask them if we could borrow some. But they said they can't give us any unless we can prove to them we're not TERRORISTS. I told them we're members of SISSY, but they didn't know what that was. I said SALAAM ALAIKUM VERY MUCH and hung up. We were stuck.

But then I BINGED it (thank you for another hundred, MACROHARD). You can pretty much find out how to do ANYTHING on the INTERTUBES. Right away, we found this WatchMeImBeggingYouTube video on how to extract deuterium from seawater.

So we were almost there. We were going to save the world from itself.

But then Fanny showed up. When he saw what we were doing to the dryer, he started bawling his eyes out. He said we wrecked the "TUM-TUMBLER." It was his favorite "MOOSMENT PARK" RIDE. It was getting late. My folks would emerge from their ZOOM caves soon. I had to distract him.

I rifled around in our pile of spare parts and found a paper clip. I told Fanny I had a new, funner ride for him to go on. It was called ELECTROSHOCK THERAPY. Guaranteed to turn his FROWN upside-down! I bent the paper clip into a tong and told him to stick it into the slitty eyes of the moon-faced little guy on the wall down there.

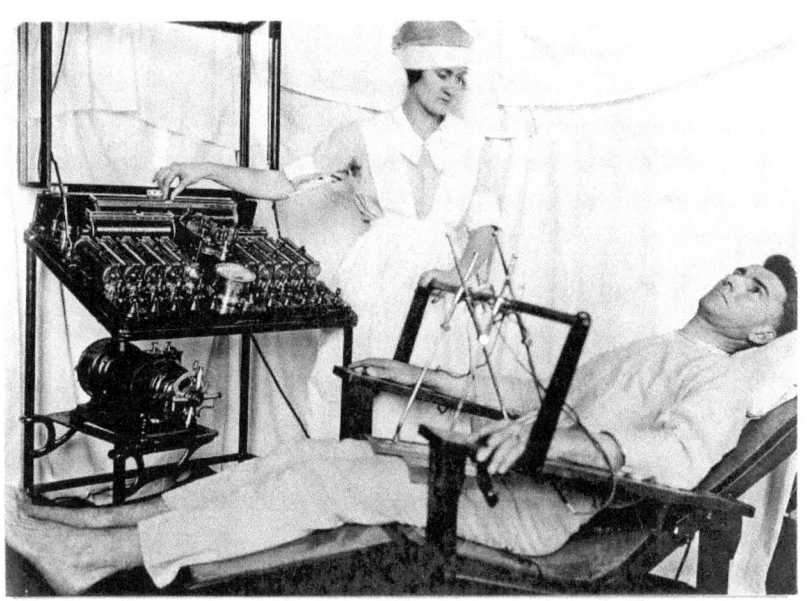

What was I thinking about? I can't remember.

But just then Pops opened the garage door. When he saw what I was up to, he got out of his pickup truck and strolled into the garage real casual-like, whistling the whole time. Whenever he acts like that I know I'm in DEEP DOO-DOO.

He took the sledgehammer off its hook and walked over to us. We all just stood there, frozen in terror. Well, actually, Fanny was FROTHING at the mouth and CONVULSING.

He walked right past Fanny, raised the sledgehammer high over his head, and brought it down on the dryer. When he'd smashed it to bits, he placed the sledgehammer carefully back on the rack and strolled up into the house, still whistling.

Finally, Fanny let go of the paper clip. He collapsed on the concrete floor with a doofy grin plastered to his chubby little face.

Jowley wanted to know what just happened. Then I remembered. Pops works for the bastard offspring of Standard Oil.

I tried to laugh the whole thing off. But Jowley was mad at ME for what POPS did. He said we should have worked on carbon sequestration all along, because that was something even the fossil fuel industry could get on board with.

We started doing that thing kids do because they don't really know how to fight. Basically, spazzing out. Shoving each other and calling each other names. Fists flailed. Spittle flew.

Right then, both of us sneezed. It looks like all the stress weakened our IMMUNE SYSTEMS. We both got the latest mutation of the VIRUS.

If Pastor Pastrychef, who runs the local megachurch, was there, I'm sure he would have said the whole situation was DIVINE JUSTICE.

WEDNESDAY

Today at school they announced there's an opening for the INFLUENCER position on the School ANTISOCIAL MEDIA feed. There's only one student slot because the School Board says they don't want to DILUTE the school brand.

Up till now, this kid with the handle StinkyTart had the job all to themself. When they started out, their posts were actually pretty good. They'd take glam shots of themself in leopard-print leotards doing twisty yoga poses. There'd be understated tie-ins for skin care products, like OVERNIGHT GLOW PEEL and MORNING SKIN SUPERPOWDER. Mostly overpriced placebos, but they made you feel so pretty and young.

But lately, StinkTart's been seriously confusing their PUBLIC and PRIVATE selves. At first, they were on the right track. They got plastic surgery, hired a trainer, and turned every interaction into a performance of authenticity, like they actually were their brand. But then they got all mushy. They told their followers to NOT be yourself, because your idea of your self was an illusion. I guess that's why some kids DOXED them.

As soon as I found out StinkyTart had been harassed into quitting, I knew I had to take their place. Antisocial media made StinkyTart a global celebrity, with over a TRILLION followers, which is much better than having, say, one close friend. I wanted to partake of that kind of NOTORIETY.

To try out, I had to come up with a few post ideas. It's easy to come up with ideas. What I do is SAMPLE ideas from Cowlick or whatever I happen to be watching or playing at the time. I twist them a little to make them my own, but not so much that kids won't know where I got them.

Using this trusted method, I was runner-up in the Social Distancing campaign the school ran during the last pandemic. I posted a snap of Jowley with a bunch of American cheese slices slapped up on his face. The tagline was, LICK ME AND GRANDMA DIES.

This kid who won first prize is named Carries Christ In His Heart Carnival Worker. What irks me is that, during pandemics, Carries Christ In His Heart goes around licking all the shampoo bottles at the local pharmacy chains.

THURSDAY

I got Jowley to join me. We agreed to be an influencer SUPERTEAM, where I do the MACHINE humor and he does the CHILD humor. That means I underreact to everything and he overreacts. And sometimes, for variety, we'll do some ANIMAL humor gags. That's when we call attention to all the funny ways people are like animals. For example, farting and burping. Or nipples. Or hairy armpits, which I haven't quite got yet.

We cranked out a bunch of setup images, but that turned out to be the easy part. When we tried to come up with some punchlines, we sank into the abyss. The machine jokes were supposed to have a sensational setup and a deadpan payoff. The child jokes had the opposite—a calm setup and a HYPERBOLIC reaction. And the animal gags, which should be the easiest to pull off, needed an uptight setup followed by a crude payoff.

But the only payoff I could think of was 💩.

It turns out poop jokes DO get old after a while. Who knew?

So I made up a series of posts where the tagline of every image is "Blue Cheese Mamba!" I thought it was particularly inspired because it was a sly ripoff of "Ay, Caramba!" That's the catchphrase of this yellow-faced eternally ten-year-old kid from a cartoon TV show. It also plays off the theme of me feeling like smelly cheese and, as a consequence, acting like a sneaky twerp.

Mummy, they stole my intellectual property.

At first, I took the photos and wrote the punchlines, while Jowley did all the modeling. But Jowley said he was tired of being

OBJECTIFIED and wanted to take his turn projecting the MALE GAZE.

Eventually I got sick of "Blue Cheese Mamba!" so I let Jowley take the pictures AND write the taglines.

It turns out Jowley is a much better photographer than me. He kept blathering on about APERTURE and DEPTH OF FIELD and EXPOSURE. I kept telling him the pictures should look really amateurish, otherwise kids'll think we're trying too hard.

Besides, I said, the camera made me look fat. The last straw was when he ordered me to tilt my torso, bend my joints, stick out my jaw, and purse my lips. MAKE LOVE TO THE CAMERA, he said.

I refuse to work with anyone who knows more than me about anything, so I told him to leave. He packed up all his gear and was halfway down the driveway when we both realized we were at his house.

FRIDAY

After Jowley left then came back, I went home and doubled down on my influencer brand. I came up with this persona called PHARMAKOS THE SCAPEGOAT. It's this character who does all these OBNOXIOUS things kind of on purpose and gets punished by the FATES so that others will enjoy a laugh at his expense. He makes them feel SUPERIOR because they would never, ever behave in such a BOORISH way.

The wilderness ain't so bad after all.

The great thing about Pharmakos the Scapegoat is that I'll never run out of primo material. All I have to do is indulge my own bottomless pit of insecurities, then foist them on everyone around me, which, luckily enough for me, is my number one talent.

When I got to school today, I showed my feed to Ms. DeVos. She's the vice principal in charge of the school's corporate outreach program.

She showed me the feeds of all the other influencers competing for the position. Most of them were really SELF-DEPRECATING, so I wasn't too worried. Everyone knows that kids my age are SELF-CENTERED in this mildly annoying way. Acting humble and self-aware gets you nowhere in middle school.

One of the influencers had the handle "Government Bad, Private Enterprise Good," which DID have me scared. It's like the kid knew exactly how to best suck up to Ms. DeVos.

Have I got a deal for you. Guaranteed to make you a bazillion bucks.

So when Ms. DeVos went out to the parking lot to get from her trunk a case of MULTI-LEVEL MARKETING toothpaste she was planning to peddle to the other teachers, I hacked into the kid's account and made a few minor edits. Every time a post used the term PRIVATIZE, I changed it to NATIONALIZE. Everywhere I found the word ENTREPRENEUR, I replaced it with PARASITIC BOURGEOISIE. And for the coup de grâce, I swapped GOD with DARWIN.

THURSDAY

During morning announcements, I was ANOINTED as the new official school influencer.

Later in class, all the kids were mindlessly scrolling through their antisocial media feeds, like they always do. I was dying to find how many LIKES and SHARES I was racking up. I knew it would be pretty hard to amass a trillion followers like StinkTart. But I figured if the school bought me a few billion bot followers here and there, I could come close.

As fate would have it, the battery on Cowlick's smartphone died, so I couldn't check my stats. Even though he was still mad at me, I convinced Jowley to let me borrow his phone. I wanted to record myself fist pumping and hooting to celebrate my achievement. It had to be spontaneous. So I waited until assembly and logged into my account right when the Principal was giving a boring lecture on the benefits of building your very own PERSONALITY CULT.

Ms. DeVos told me she'd made a few minor edits to my posts. But she totally wrecked them. Instead of having Fate punish

Pharmakos the Scapegoat's HUBRIS, he was rewarded. Any time he did something cruel and obnoxious, he wasn't held responsible. Instead, the MEDIA or IMMIGRANTS or FOREIGNERS or the DEEP STATE were blamed.

The kids loved it. My followers were growing EXPONENTIALLY. That's a math term. I usually tune out during Math class, but for some reason, this idea stuck. It means that if you're infected with a contagious disease and you spread it to two people every day, in a week, the universe will EXPLODE.

It wasn't exactly the message for my brand I had in mind. But, hey, winning is the only thing that matters, right?

So now all of sudden, I'm, like, the most popular kid in school. Not only in school, but soon the whole world. While the world burns, I BLEW UP.

MARCH

WEDNESDAY

Being the most popular kid in school is a ROYAL PAIN IN THE ASS. At first, I thought it'd be cool to be surrounded by a bunch of FANS, YES MEN, BUTT KISSERS, BOOTLICKERS, GROUPIES, DOORMATS, BACKSLAPPERS, GLAD HANDERS, FAWNERS, FLUNKIES, TOADIES, and SYCOPHANTS. But when everybody around you always agrees with you, lavishes praise on you, and tells you what a genius you are, your thinking starts to go a bit wonky.

The thing is—when you finally get something you've wished for your whole life—you feel pretty EUPHORIC about it for a while. But the euphoria wears off. Then you feel really empty. You realize that the thing you were convinced would bring you ETERNAL HAPPINESS doesn't. Can't. Because lasting happiness doesn't come from CHANGING CIRCUMSTANCE.

When you realize this, your whole sense of self is screwed. All that SEEKING to puff your SELF up strikes you as pretty pointless. So now what?

While I was pondering the ABYSS in Social Studies, an announcement came over the loudspeaker.

Jowley had to report to Mr. Naryshkin in his office in the basement. When he came back an hour later, he was bruised up and had a black eye.

Apparently, Mr. Naryshkin got a text from one of his moles in SISSY. If you're not familiar, moles are spies who spy on spies. Because you can't trust anybody these days, am I right?

They reported having witnessed Jowley "traumatizing" the eighth-graders we were supposed to be spying on. Mr. Naryshkin told him he'd violated the SACRED CODE of SISSY, which was to fake camaraderie to gain trust.

I know exactly what this is all about. Last week, when Jowley and I were fighting, I hung out with the eighth-graders, who now all think I'm AWESOME. While they were sucking up to me, I let slip that the economy was about to tank. We were facing a deep recession that would last years. Their prospects for getting a college degree, a white-collar job, and a living wage were now next to zilch. Their only real hope of making it in this new world order was to become a LOYAL INSTRUMENT OF THE STATE or, at the very least, the PERSONAL ASSISTANT TO A BILLIONAIRE.

Since I'm a public figure now, Mr. Naryshkin can't punish me. So he decided to express his disapproval of my behavior by punishing the person he thought was my best friend.

I knew I should probably come up with a scheme to crush Mr. Naryshkin. But if I got caught, the administration might lock me out of my official school influencer account. Then I'd be a NOBODY again.

No one wants that for me. So I thought it would be wiser to let Jowley take the fall on my behalf. I can pay him back later by giving him a guest post or re-gifting some free swag to him or something like that.

At dinner, Mummy sensed that something was troubling me. She wheedled me all through the main course—dead animal flesh pumped full of growth hormones and antibiotics with a side serving of processed starch—about the juicy details. Finally, she promised me a double-serving of my favorite dessert—high fructose corn syrup—if I spilled the beans. So I did.

When I was done confessing, she offered some advice. She said all stories are bulltucky because they foster, through the literary device of characters driving plot, the illusion that selves make choices that define them.

In fact, she said, I should stop trying to do anything, because our choices don't make us who we are. On the contrary, 99% of our choices are just the product of conditioning. If you consider carefully the nature of thought, you'll discover that who you think you are isn't who you really are. The so-called "I" doesn't actually choose anything. Therefore, doing the "right" or "wrong" thing based on who you think you are just perpetuates suffering.

At the time, it sounded like great advice. But I'm pretty sure I'm going to forget it by tomorrow, get caught up in thinking, then act on what I believe is a choice.

THURSDAY

For some reason, I slept like a baby last night. In the morning, I decided to do nothing. But doing nothing is still doing something—the absence of something.

After school, I told Jowley his resentment toward me was just thought. He should forget about it. Think about something else. Something shiny and happy. Plus, the bruises would eventually heal.

I asked him if he wanted to practice our waterboarding techniques at his house. He said he couldn't because he was going to a meeting. I asked him if I could tag along. He said definitely not.

When I got home, Mummy was waiting for me in the kitchen. She didn't say anything. She just offered me an IV bag full of high fructose corn syrup.

TUESDAY

The Principal called me into his office this morning. When I got there, the President was with him, along with the Secretary General of the United Nations, as well as all the other leaders of the G20.

I kind of knew this was inevitable.

Because I was so wonderful, the United Nations had unanimously voted to make me KING OF THE WORLD.

Almost there.

THURSDAY

It's been fun to treat everybody in the world like a plaything. For a while. But the thrill's worn off, just like it did with being the most popular kid in school.

I've realized the only way to guarantee my happiness is to figure out a way to make myself OMNIPOTENT, like an A List Superhero.

No. That isn't going to be enough. I have to make myself not only all-powerful, but also IMMORTAL, like a god.

But how am I going to do that? All the latest scientific and technological advancements at my fingertips fall woefully short. The vast power of human civilization is trifling compared to the power I longed for.

If you were in my sneakers, what would you do? How can I guarantee the security of my SELF? How can I gratify all my desires, while also permanently banishing all of my fears? How can I arrange my inner- and outer-circumstances always and exactly as I want them to be?

Then it hit me. The imagination. I can tell myself a story so convincingly that the story is, for me, real. Since I'm the storyteller, I'll be all-powerful. Then I can live happily ever after. Or, at least, for as long as the story captivates me. When it no longer does, I'll move onto the next story. AD INFINITUM.

Next, I'll have to convince everyone around me to buy into my story. That shouldn't be too hard.

This is going to be the greatest scam of my life so far.

I'll start with Jowley.

FRIDAY

I discovered a big problem with my plan. Whenever I start to get all cozy inside one of the stories I tell myself, reality keeps intruding.

For example, Jowley's been hanging out with Token Minority Kid lately. It makes me sick. Not that Token is brown. It's that I'm jealous. Token is supposed to be my WHITE-GUILT SALVE, not Jowley's.

To get back at him, I decided to make him jealous back by being best friends with Freckly. He's the only one I know who's too clueless to suck up to me because of my high social status. Freckly is like the COURT JESTER who speaks TRUTH TO POWER.

When I showed up at his double-wide, the first thing Freckly said to me was that I wasn't really disgusted by him, just afraid of him. That wasn't because he was much lower than me in the school social hierarchy, but because his family was WORKING CLASS.

On top of that, unlike me, he's not disgusted by his own body, so he's willing to be physically close in ways that I'm not, like playing Tangled Spaghetti or Spin-the-Bottle with another boy.

Up in his room with the door locked, Freckly asked me if I'd like a back rub. That's when I really got the heebie-jeebies.

In other versions of this story, I write that Freckly stole the candy in my Henri (that's pronounced AHN-REE, you plebe) Versailles duffel bag. But actually I whipped out an IV full of high fructose corn syrup and gave it to him, even though I was warned by his mom that he has TYPE II DIABETES.

Freckly mainlined the whole bag. Then he started to shake all over and babble. It wasn't long before he was writhing on the floor, speaking in tongues, and proclaiming that he'd seen the LIZARD KING.

I decided the best course of action was to get the heck out of there. I climbed out the window and ran home. On the way, I heard ambulance sirens.

MAY

MONDAY

Oh, yeah, the rest of my story of a middle grade school year.

I could tell you that me and Jowley got back together. And that it was because I had this flash of insight about my character flaws and made this big sacrifice for him.

But that would be pretty lame. Kind of like a DEUS EX MACHINA who descends onto the stage at the end of an ancient comedy to tidy up a messy plot. That means GOD OUT OF THE MACHINE.

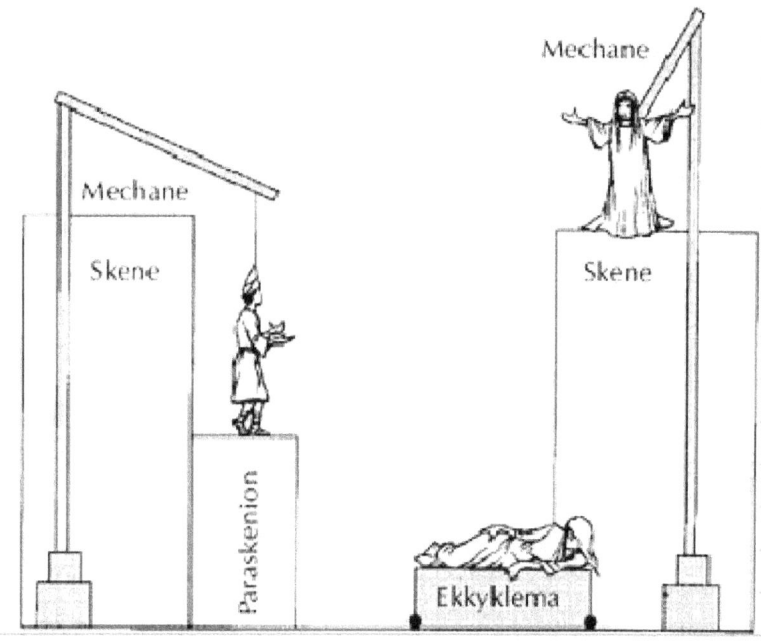

But this plot isn't so messy, like I said earlier. Just a series of episodes where my scams get foiled and I don't learn much until, as if my magic, at the very end, I get what friendship is kinda-sorta all about.

And all the while, you, the reader, enjoy a few cheap laughs at my expense by bearing witness to my mostly harmless but deeply troubled shenanigans.

But I already told you I was made KING OF THE WORLD. What do I care about Jowley's friendship? I have more followers now that I can handle. They're constantly telling me how wonderful I am.

It's funny. In that other version of my story, I contrived to have some teenagers force Jowley to eat the slice of moldy cheese on the four square court. As I told you earlier, that cheese, however preposterous, was a symbol of my shame. In a way, then, Jowley figuratively ATE my shame. Then I took credit with our classmates for its disappearance from the court.

Which was the bigger sacrifice?

Shortly thereafter, in recognition of some trifling accomplishment, Jowley got IMMORTALIZED in the yearbook with some VACUOUS SOBRIQUET. So he turned out in the end to be more popular than me. All because he was nice. How IRONICAL.

And since I did him that tiny favor, he allowed me to be his sidekick again.

Big-whoop. Everybody knows that in a just society the person who is the most generous to others rises to the top of the pecking order.

But we don't live in a just society, do we? And trying to change it through actions based on choices only perpetuates the injustice.

So what's a poor boy to do?

Escape into the labyrinth of stories and be the MASTER OF THE UNIVERSE there, that's what.

Now that I've won the championship, I'm going to DIZZKNEE world.

About the Author

Jest Ninney is a virtual goat herder, and a #1 *New Jerk Times* worstselling author. In 1819, the *Anti-Jacobin Review* presciently named Jest one of the 100 Least Influential People of the Future. He pissed away his childhood in Jerberbia and moved completely into his own head in 1999 to avoid Y2K. Jest still lives there with his blowup spouse and his goats.

www.ingramcontent.com/pod-product-compliance
Lightning Source LLC
Chambersburg PA
CBHW070558180626
46817CB00005B/1892